CHILDREN OF HEAVEN

CHRISTIANE ROCHEFORT

CHILDREN
OF
HEAVEN

True life is absent.
—RIMBAUD

Translated from the French by
LINDA ASHER

David McKay Company, Inc.

New York

CHILDREN OF HEAVEN

COPYRIGHT © 1962 BY DAVID MCKAY COMPANY, INC.

PUBLISHED SIMULTANEOUSLY IN THE DOMINION OF CANADA

First Edition

Library of Congress Catalog Card Number: 62-15776

MANUFACTURED IN THE UNITED STATES OF AMERICA

VAN REES PRESS • NEW YORK

CHILDREN OF HEAVEN

Chapter 1

I WAS BORN OF THE FAMILY
Subsidies and a holiday morning stretching comfortably to
the tune of "I love you and you love me" played on a sweet
horn. It was early winter, the bed felt good, there was no
hurry.

In the middle of July my parents went to the hospital.
My mother was having pains. They examined her and they
told her it wasn't time yet. My mother insisted she was
having pains. It would take a good two weeks more, the
nurse said; she should tighten up her girdle.

But couldn't they register the birth now anyway? my father asked. And what would they register, the nurse said —a girl, a boy, a calf? We were sent right back home.

Nuts, my father said what lousy luck, we'll miss out on the bonus by two weeks. He looked resentfully at his wife's belly. That was that. They took the métro home. Water, water everywhere, and not a drop for them to drink.

I was born the second of August. That was my due date, since I came from the All Saints' weekend. But they always thought of me as late. Besides, I had made them lose out on vacation, by keeping them in Paris while the factory was closed. I couldn't do anything right.

Actually, though, I was early at most things: Patrick had barely taken over my place in the cradle when I learned to get out of the room, holding on, the minute he started bawling. In a way I could say it was Patrick who taught me to walk.

When the twins were finally given back to us, after shunting around a long time in various hospitals—at least we assumed the ones who came were ours, it was some pair of boy twins anyway—I was already dressing myself and I could hoist things up onto the table—the dishes, the salt, the bread, the mustard tube—and tell the different napkins in their rings. Grow up fast, my mother would say, so you can give me a hand.

She was already a wreck when I first knew her; she had a dropped womb, she couldn't go to the factory for more than a week at a time, because she had to work standing up. After Chantal was born she stopped altogether, there was no point; this way they would have the Single Salary allotment, for what she earned not to mention the rigama-role with the Social Security every time she had a Work

Interruption, and with all she'd have to do now at home with five tiny little babies to take care of, they figured out that it wasn't worth it, at least not if the baby lived.

I could already help out quite a bit by then, go for the bread, push the twins around the Project in their double carriage to give them some fresh air, keep an eye on Patrick who was precocious too, unfortunately. He was still under three years old when he stuck a baby kitten into the washing machine. For once at least papa gave him a real licking; the machine wasn't even paid off yet.

Chantal survived finally, thanks to such a fantastic treatment that the old lady was always amazed at the thought of it and never got tired of telling the tale to the other hens, and about how she had screamed when she saw her little girl lying there stark naked in the middle of big chunks of ice, and how the doctor told her there was no other way to save her, and he was right, it did. After all that Chantal was a kind of favorite with her, if you could talk about favorites in her case; anyhow she took care of her herself, whereas the others were left to me, including Catherine later on, even when she was still a tiny baby.

I started school. Mornings I would give the boys breakfast, I would drop them at the day nursery, and go on to school. Lunchtime I would stay in and go to the canteen. I liked the canteen, you sat down and the plate would come to you all filled up; whatever comes on a plate that's already filled it always tastes good. Most of the other girls didn't like the canteen, they thought it was no good; I wondered what they ate at home. When I asked them, though, it was the same as we had, the same brands, from the same stores, except for the mustard, papa would bring that home right from the factory. We put mustard in everything.

[3]

After school I would bring the boys home and leave them downstairs in the court to play with the other kids. I would go up for money and then back down to do the marketing. Mama would make dinner, papa would come home and turn on the TV, we would eat, papa and the boys would watch TV, mama and I did the dishes, and then they all went to bed. I would stay on in the kitchen, doing my homework.

We had a good apartment now. Before, we lived in the 13th *arrondissement*, one lousy room with the toilet on the landing. When that section was torn down we were relocated here, we had priority; Large Families had priority in this Project. We got the number of rooms we were entitled to according to the number of children. The parents had one bedroom, the boys had another one, I slept with the babies in the third; we had a bathroom, the washing machine came when the twins were born, and there was a kitchen-parlor where we ate; I did my homework in the kitchen, where the table was.

That was my favorite time—what a pleasure when they had all cleared out and left me alone in the night and the silence. During the day I never heard the racket, I ignored it; but at night I could hear the silence. The silence started at ten o'clock. The radios stopped, the squalling, the voices, the clink of dishes in the sink; one by one the windows would go black. At ten-thirty it was all finished. Nothing. A desert. I was alone. Oh, how calm and peaceful all around me, everyone asleep, the windows dark except for one or two where someone else was staying up like me, alone, quiet, enjoying his peace! After a while I got to like doing homework. The sound of papa's big snores through the wall, meaning he had nothing to worry about for a while; every now and then some noise from the babies' room, Chantal choking from lying on her stomach, Catherine having a nightmare; I would just shift them around a little and everything was all right again, I could go back to my table.

People were always talking about how much I loved my brothers and sisters, how I was a regular little mommy. The old hens would see me go by, pushing Catherine, pulling Chantal, yelling after the boys, and they would tell my mother I was "a regular little mommy." When they said it they would lean toward me with their faces all mushy as if they were about to melt and I would move back to get out of the way. The hens were loaded with ailments which they never stopped talking about in full detail, especially in the gut, and everyone else they knew was sick too.

Most of them had tumors, and they were always wondering whether it was cancer or not; when it was cancer the person would die and they would collect for a wreath. Mama had no tumor, she had albumin and now that she was pregnant she had to go absolutely without salt, which made things all the more complicated, because we had to cook two different meals.

When the baby died at birth, I don't think I really felt very sorry. Just that it was funny seeing her come back home from the hospital with nothing that time. She couldn't get used to it herself either, she didn't know what to do with herself, and meanwhile the work piled up around her. Then little by little she began to get back to normal, and after a while we all forgot about the poor baby.

Chantal was walking by then and starting to talk, she would tug mama by the dress and keep asking "Whe' lil brud? Whe' lil brud?" They had promised her one. "Ah leave me alone for god's sakes," my mother would answer the way she always did, "you wear me out! Here, give me your nose let me wipe it. Blow." Chantal had a cold; in the wintertime she was nothing but one long cold from start to finish with maybe a bronchitis or a little sinusitis now and then just for a change. The twins had whooping cough that year.

To keep Chantal quiet I told her the little Brother couldn't come right now, there weren't enough cabbages, but he would certainly come the next time.

"Don't tempt fate," mama said, "I got enough head-aches with the rest of you."

The store came to take back the TV because we couldn't keep up the payments. Mama explained that it was because the baby died, that it certainly wasn't her fault he didn't live, and with her health the way it was things were already pretty sad and now if she couldn't even have the TV; they took the thing away anyhow, and on top of it all when papa came home he began to holler that she let them step on her. Those bastards he said they came around begging you to take their lousy junk, they practically tell you they're giving it to you free and then the least little bit overdue they turn around and take it back; if he had been home we'd still have the damn thing.

Oh sure you're pretty smart, she told him, anyone could see that from the way we live, and that started them off again blaming each other for everything since the day they met.

Things were pretty bad. They were counting every last penny.

I don't know how you do it, papa said, I just don't know

how you do it, and mama said she would manage a lot better if there was no such thing as horse races. Papa said the pari-mutuel didn't cost a cent, with the wins and losses it balanced out and besides he only played it once in a while and if he couldn't have even this one little pleasure then what would he have, life wasn't such a ball as it was. And what about me, what do I have? she said, I don't have a thing, not a blessed bit of fun anytime in this stinking life working from morning till night just so his lordship can find everything just right when he comes home to stick his legs under the table, Shit said his lordship That's the least after a whole day pushing that mustard crap into tubes like a damn fool and getting home knocked out after an hour and a half trip standing up if he at least had a car it would be a little easier Oh this is just the time to talk about a car she said oh a real fine time! When we can't even get the TV back and Patrick needing shoes with those feet of his that never quit growing. It's not my fault Patrick said, You keep out of this papa told him it's none of your business, But my feet hurt Patrick said Are you going to shut your mouth yes or no? Without the TV at night they didn't know what to do with themselves, they'd pick a fight over anything and everything. Papa would take longer over his drink on the way home, mama would bawl him out, he would answer he was in no hurry to get home just for the fun of hearing her complaints, and off they went again. The kids would start screaming, we'd get hit over nothing.

I hate a scene. The noise it makes and the time it takes up. I would boil inside, just waiting for them to wear themselves out and go to bed, and leave me alone in my kitchen, in peace.

*　　*　　*　　*　　*

One day a lady came around asking if the children went to catechism. It was a Thursday, after lunch, no school, I was dressing the kids to take them out. Mama was ironing; the lady started telling her about the advantages of sending the children to catechism. Mama had no opinion one way or the other; the lady said if Patrick belonged to the Cubs he would go on outings Thursdays and Sundays. Mama unplugged the iron; she asked her if the twins were big enough to go along on those outings Thursdays and Sundays. But she needed me around. The lady explained I wouldn't have to belong to the youth group, just go to catechism one hour a week, after school. Mama didn't know, she would have to ask my father. I finished buttoning Chantal's coat. I said "I'd like that, going to catechism."

My mother gaped at me. The lady gave me such a smile I nearly changed my mind. She looked like a piece of cream cheese.

They couldn't think of any reason why not. "Well all right that's settled," mama said.

Mondays when I got out of school I would turn left instead of right, and I would come home an hour and a half later, when everything was done. It was worth it.

The teacher opened the book and said, "What is God? God is a pure spirit, infinitely perfect."

Never in my whole life had I ever heard such a strange thing. God is a pure spirit infinitely perfect. What could it be? I sat there with my mouth open. I lost track of what came after. I woke up to hear the teacher asking, in a louder voice, "What is God?" and looking at us with a very stern face.

"God is a pure spirit infinitely perfect," the others answered calmly. I couldn't say it along with them, I didn't understand the sentence, not a single word of it. It was a bad start.

The lesson ended. I had hardly heard a word of it. I got up like all the rest of them, I walked back home, thinking hard.

I don't know what went on in the house that night, who yelled, or at whom, what we ate, or what became of the dishes. I was turning the sentence over and over in my head, trying to figure out how to take hold of it, and I couldn't do it. The pure spirit infinitely perfect stuck in my head, white, smooth, closed off like an egg. I fell asleep without managing to crack it.

Mademoiselle Garret didn't lay an egg every week. In general, aside from sacred history which was nicer than nonsacred history, and one thing, there were no dates, it was a bunch of complicated, boring explanations like "if it takes a workman to build a house, it must have taken a God to create heaven and earth." Well, there, I couldn't see why really, and I had some trouble with Mademoiselle Garret, who couldn't understand why I couldn't understand, and told me I was being "argumentative." It was a funny kind of discussion, I wasn't the one who was being argumentative, it was them with their workman. But when people are set on something there's nothing you can do. She told me I didn't have to try to understand, I was just supposed to learn it by heart, that's all they were asking me to do. But I can't memorize something I don't understand, it's like trying to swallow a Brillo pad. I was getting fed up, Mademoiselle Garret said I was being too independent, and if it hadn't been for the walk home all by myself I would have dropped it when she told us one day "Man is composed of a body and a soul."

[9]

Mystery. There it was, all over again. I left the details for the others to fool with, and I contemplated my second egg; it seemed a little plainer than the first one, at least as far as the grammer. But the meaning wasn't. Man is composed of a body and a soul. What about me?

"Josyane? Well, Josyane, dreaming?"

"Does everybody have a soul?"

"Of course," said Mademoiselle Garret, shrugging her shoulders slightly. I would have asked some other questions but Mademoiselle Garret didn't like that, she would get irritated right away. I carried my second egg away with me. So I had a soul, like everybody else, Mademoiselle Garret had been definite about that. In a way, even though I wasn't too sure exactly what it was, it didn't surprise me all that much.

On catechism days Ethel Lefranc, who didn't go, would pick up Chantal at the nursery at the same time she went for her own little brother; the boys could get along by themselves now, all I had to do was stop for them at the playground on my way back.

It was dark. Almost all the windows were lighted up in the big new apartment houses on the other side of the avenue. More and more of those apartments had people living in them now. A building got finished and bang it was filled up.

I had watched them being built. Now they were nearly full. Long, tall, set on the flat plain like that, they made me think of ships. The wind blew across the level ground between the houses. I like going through there. It was big, and beautiful, and terrible. When I walked right close to them, I felt as though they were going to fall over on me.

Everybody looked minute next to them, and even the buildings in our project looked like toy blocks beside them. The people scurried around like little bugs under the street lights. Voices and radio noises came out from the houses, I could see and hear it all, I felt very far away and a little sick to my stomach, or in fact maybe it was in that soul. I picked up the kids. I went home.

"Go on back down quick and get the milk, I didn't have time, Chantal has a temperature again, that kid it's always something. There's money on the buffet. Take the garbage down when you go, and get some grated cheese and a bread, remember to bring in the stroller on your way back and look and see if there's any mail while you're there, hurry up your father'll be home any minute, you should have been back already."

If Mademoiselle Garret was right she had a soul too, I would have asked but ma went into the hospital and I quit catechism for a while and afterwards it slipped my mind. Nicolas was born in February, before he was due.

For a while there I had thought it was all over, she was sick since the dead baby, and I even thought maybe she had had them take everything out at the time, she'd been talking about doing it for so long. Everyone was growing up, even Catherine managed to button herself up in spite of being retarded, I was looking forward to the day not too far off when they would all be able to get along on their own, and I wouldn't have anything left to do; and now it was starting all over again from zero.

With the money that would be coming in for Nicolas they could get the washing machine overhauled and that was a good thing because otherwise the diapers, and I was sick of diapers, really sick. They could get the TV back, which suited me fine, too, because when it was in the house things were a lot more peaceful. Then after that, with a little luck, they could maybe think about the car. That was what they were aiming for now, instead of the fridge, mama would have liked a fridge but papa said it was his turn for a little comfort, not always his wife's, he was so worn out with the trip from one suburb to another he was beginning to have a bellyful. Mama could just go right on marketing every day, in fact I was the one who went, they didn't seem to think about that. They spent a whole evening figuring out about that car thing, whether they could do it with the Subsidy, scraping a little here and there, plus the tax and minus the TV payments, and if she could make a little extra on a couple of cleaning jobs and still stay under the limit for the Single Salary allotment, the social worker had given them all the figures, what would throw the whole thing out the window would be having to buy a new bed for Catherine if Nicolas went into the crib, a bed is expensive. They spread out their papers all over my table, in my way; they spoiled my whole evening, it's a good thing it didn't happen every day.

Finally Uncle Georges came—he liked to putter, not like papa who couldn't do a thing with his ten fingers—he put up a little bed on top of Chantal's. She would climb up a story, and Catherine would get out of the crib and move into the ground floor, and what would we do next, the ceiling would never be high enough if they kept on coming. That way there was only the mattress left to buy.

Mama wanted to leave Chantal down below, in her old bed—"She's so delicate." She might fall down and break.

But Catherine was still pretty small, and dumb the way she was she could easily dive out and split her head open.

Catherine refused to leave her old bed. She hung onto it and when I pulled her the bed came too. You could hear her screaming through the whole house. There were three of us working on her. Patrick, who was drawn by the smell of blood, refereed the battle: "Go on, Cathy, give it to them! Don't let 'em push you around!" Papa really lost his temper and smacked him, which as usual made him laugh. "What are we going to do with him, really what are we going to do with him," mama moaned, "my god what are we going to do I ask you what are we going to do with him what are we going to do ah what in god's name we going to do with that kid!"

Patrick said Ksss Ksss and Catherine got excited again and kicked and bit us. The neighbors were banging on the wall, it was ten o'clock.

When the battle was over it was a victory for Catherine. Nicolas would be in the incubator for another three weeks anyway, so why bother fighting now. We could play the next half when he arrived, and maybe he'd die before that, which would settle everything. We were all exhausted. Only the twins had kept out of it, they never mixed into our squabbles; they were asleep in their bed, clasped sweetly in each other's arms.

I took over my kitchen again and opened my notebook. For a minute I heard my mother groaning in the next room—"Oh la la am I tired, oh, how tired I am they'll kill me; they'll be the death of me those kids, I'm worn out, oh my god I'm knocked out and that's the truth oh, la, oh my god am I tired." Papa was already snoring into the dark night. The springs creaked, she was climbing into bed. A sigh. Silence. Relief. Peace.

"The handkerchief you gave me when I won the cross is white." The handkerchief—you gave me—when I won the cross—is white.

The handkerchief is white: main clause; *the*: definite article; *handkerchief*: common noun, singular, subject of verb *is*; *is*: third person singular, present indicative of the verb *to be*; *white*: adjective modifying *handkerchief*.

You gave me: subordinate clause, complementing *handkerchief*; *which*: subordinate conjunction, understood; *you*: personal pronoun, second person singular, subject of the verb *gave*; *me*: personal pronoun, first person singular, indirect object of verb *gave*.

The longer an assignment was, the more I liked it. The pen would scratch away in the silence. I liked that. I liked the pen, the paper, even the five little lines you had to fit the letters into; and the worst assignments, long division, the rule of three; and most of all I liked diagramming sentences. I really got a bang out of that. The other girls said it was useless. That didn't bother me. In fact I think the more useless it was the better I liked it. I would have liked to spend my whole life doing things that were useless.

Gave: past tense of the verb *to give*, second person singular.

The teacher would tell me "There's no need to put so much down, Josyane; just try not to leave any silly mistakes in, that's more important." Because I did make mistakes, and I usually came out just average; but then I wasn't trying to be first. It didn't matter to me. On the whole I didn't much care what people thought of me. In my report card the teacher wrote "equally indifferent to praise and blame," but since nobody ever looked at the card she might just as well have written it's springtime, or Toto loves Zizi, or this girl is a deadhead; it wouldn't have made any difference. Once the year before I was third in the class, I don't know why, it just happened that way, all the others must have been sick; I stuck the card right under papa's nose that time, he looked at it and gave it back to me, saying "Good." Just in case he had missed that column I said "I'm third." That got me "Oh good." Period, I didn't give a damn what he thought anyhow.

As long as we were off in school and out of the way, that was all they cared about. When Patrick got himself kicked out, for instance, that made them mad: "So you'll hang around here in my way the whole damn day long?" No sir. All right, we could live as long as we were there already—but do it somewhere else, as far away as possible. Will you get out and leave me alone, are you finished asking questions, give me a little peace, you'll hang around in my way the whole damn day long. Bingo she was off like a shot to the school, phlebitis or not, and they took Patrick back in, You understand I don't have the time to spend on him, to keep an eye on him. If he didn't straighten out they would send him to the Correctional. That Correctional was a real find; that time Patrick got scared and he steered just straight enough not to get thrown out again. Delighted with the results, they applied the same technique with Cathy: "If you don't quiet down you'll go to the Shelter for Backward Children." They were beginning to get the hang of education. Cathy was four, she didn't know what the Shelter was. Patrick explained it to her: he twisted up his face every whichway and drooled and made noises in his throat, to show her what they were like there. Cathy howled. She dreamed about it at night, I would have to go wake her up; she would crouch against the wall, with her big eyes bulging out of her head. Whenever she heard the word Shelter she clutched up. Patrick was even better at educational method than the parents.

Shit on Patrick. Let him go play paratroopers with his gang down by the old man's shack still standing there in the old section, behind the Project, in the little lot full of all-colored hollyhocks in June; he can go play with what's left of the tree there, they broke practically all of its branches building some lousy little hut that doesn't even stand up straight, and they tear it down before it's even finished, and then they go and break off more branches so they can build another hut to tear down. I never saw anything as stupid as those boys. Or else they stick an old tarp over pieces of wood, and go inside it to play "jail": that was a game where they would catch people going by, who weren't too big of course, and take them inside the tent and give them the third degree. It didn't work with the twins though; it's not easy to catch two from behind at a time, when Patrick jumped one of them the other would climb all over him, and he would have to give up, like the day they got him down and were pounding him with rocks. Some guy from the Project who was walking by pulled him out from under; the man dragged the twins home by the ears and called them little bastards. Right off I said to myself Patrick must have really given it to them first. "Any more of that," mama said, "you'll all go to the Correctional." Onward with the Method. "That way I'll get a little peace." There were times when I'd even have volunteered for the Correctional myself. I cleaned Patrick's face up with alcohol; he made it a point of honor not to wince, trying to impress god knows who, nobody gave a damn. Chantal began to throw up. Blood, she couldn't stand the sight of it. Not a word from Catherine; she was over in the corner grinning vaguely and fiddling with herself. I smeared Patrick with mercurochrome; he looked more like a paratrooper than ever. Mama pulled the potatoes off the stove. They had stuck while she was holding Chantal's head. Thursdays, beautiful Thursdays.

"Here," she told me, "peel some more. You two clear out of here, and no more of your dumb tricks, tracking people in here where it's none of their business."

"Pati! Pati!"

Catherine was calling her brother, about an hour too late; he had already taken off to show his pals the glorious face of a wounded hero, and to plot revenge.

"Leave it," my mother said to me, "you're peeling off more than you're leaving. With prices what they are."

I didn't answer; I usually didn't, I waited for it to pass. I waited for the day to pass, I waited for evening, the evening would always come eventually, no fighting it, and the night, the night would get them all, mow them down like ripe wheat, lay them out for the count, and then I would be alone. Alone. Alone. I won out in the end.

Chapter 2

Nicolas left his incubator and came home just as spring began.

At the time I noticed the buds on the trees, and the green shoots. So it was the real thing.

This time the little chestnut tree was dead though, it would never grow back; they had finally killed it off. They put ropes around it, and pulled till it broke. Why didn't someone make lumbermen out of them, instead of packers, finishers, welders, mustardmakers? Three of the little trees in the courtyard—in the beginning the court was called "the

Park Area"—would never grow again either; they liked hanging off them and bending them down to the ground. The one who could bend it down lowest was the big man. Since we moved in they had killed off twelve that way. Once I caught Patrick doing it and I yelled at him.

"Leave him alone, at least while he's doing that he keeps out of trouble," my mother said.

On the bureau in their bedroom there was a snapshot from around the time they were married. They were on a motor bike, she had long hair and a big skirt all spread out; they were laughing. She could have been some girl like the ones I saw nowadays at the gate, waiting to be picked up for a ride on a scooter. You wouldn't have thought it was our parents.

Her skin was dried out now, and what did she do to her hair, to lose half of it like that? She looked straight ahead, at nothing. As hard as I tried, I just couldn't believe it was the same girl, on the motor bike.

Now that she had quit the factory she did the stairways in the Project. It brought in just enough not to lose the Single Salary allotment, they figured it out. Chantal would follow her like a puppy. Catherine wandered around, usually not too far from Patrick, with a couple of other kids the same age, all busy throwing stones. When they could find a cat or a dog they had a ball, but that was rare, animals never lasted long here. Once I saw them kicking the daylights out of some poor mutt who was hanging around like a fool, and I told them the dogs would come after them sometime and bite off their feet, at night when they were all alone in the house with their mother dying in the hospital. I really piled it on, inventing things, but a lot of good it did—they stared at me with that completely dead look the kids around here have sometimes; when I ran out of ideas and stopped talking they calmly went back to kicking him again. I saw red and I smacked Catherine twice—Catherine, because she was my sister, but I really wanted to whack one of them against the other. Right away some lady came shooting out of the apartment house like a lunatic and called me a savage, beating up little children. I told her they were scum and she should go to hell. That raised a fuss. My mother told me "Just don't butt into things that are none of your business, he wasn't your dog, was he?" As she says while they're doing that they keep out of trouble, and at least they're not in the way.

By that time Nicolas was the only one still home. I took care of him when I wasn't at school.

He was pale and redheaded and he had kept his light eyes, the others had brown ones, not to mention the twins of course who were as dark as prunes and real curly-haired but those twins were a mystery anyway.

Mama hardly spent any time on Nicolas at all; I was big now, she could rely on me. He was no bother, he didn't make much noise. He watched everything with his wide light eyes, looking as though he wondered what kind of bughouse he had fallen into, and why. I thought he might have a soul. I almost killed Catherine when I caught her sticking her fingers into his eyes, the way kids do. I took hold of her skinny little mop of hair and moved my fingers slowly toward her bulging eyes, like in a movie. She screeched; naturally Patrick came running. "They'll put you in the Shelter for Blind and Backward Children," he said. Catherine had a fit practically and I left her kicking and screaming on the floor. It didn't stop her anyway. But really nobody has a right to be so mean when they're so ugly.

I would talk to Nicolas the way I always did to the babies when I was alone taking care of them, but with him it seemed like he was listening, and that encouraged me; I would tell him everything that happened to me, or when I was mad about something, or anything at all; he loved me to take care of him, he would curl up in my hands and laugh. I felt better talking to him.

Once I got to be friends with a girl, Fatima. We met one night when she was trying to round up her brothers to go home and I was doing the same with mine. She pointed to the twins and asked me "Are those two yours? I would never have guessed it." Nobody believed it, it always took some doing to convince them. Fatima asked me how many I had: three. "I've got four," she said, counting them off. I said, But I have two girls besides. I've got three, she said, and two that died. I have only one that died, I said, and I have a baby too, named Nicolas. We're going to have another one in July, she said. We counted up the score; she won. We laughed. But we couldn't stay long, there was work waiting for us at home. She collected her brothers; all of them were dark and kinky-haired like my twins.

I had no friends at school; I don't like girls, they're stupid. Fatima was different, we had things to talk about. I saw her after that. But we never really had time, it was always her going off on errands, me coming back, or vice versa. And that was too bad because I really liked her. It always made me glad to see her coming from a distance, with all that black hair and that smile. We understood each other, Fatima and I. But she went away, they moved to the big development at Nanterre, because they didn't have room enough here any more, there were eleven of them in three rooms. I told Nicolas that Fatima had left. I was sad.

Each night when I went in to sleep I would find him sitting up in his bed. I never turn on the light to get undressed, so as not to wake the kids up, but when the moon is out you can see everything bright as day in the bedroom; Nicolas never went to sleep before I came in to talk to him and kiss him good night and I liked seeing him there waiting for me, and feeling him all warm and soft against me.

One day at school the teacher told us a fable about a king who had some secret he wasn't supposed to tell anyone. Finally when he couldn't hold it in any more, he lay down in the reeds and told it to them. But the reeds told the wind, and the wind told everyone else.

I thought it was a very good fable, but my luck, when the teacher asked me what the king's secret was, I just couldn't remember. Well, she said, he would have been better off telling it to you, and she gave me a zero to teach me to listen in class.

I told Nicolas the fable that night. When he sits there straight up, white and redheaded, shining in the moonlight, whatever I tell him becomes something beautiful; I said I'm the king and you're the reeds. I kissed him.

Catherine tosses around having bad dreams; Chantal, puny as she is, she snores as hard as papa, her nose is always so stuffed. The minute I kiss him, Nicolas falls asleep like an angel, and doesn't move for the rest of the night.

At two and a half years old he still didn't talk. Not even mama, papa. That finally surprised even them. They tried to make him talk, say mama, papa, pa pa pa . . . Nothing. Peepee. He would stare at them with a dumb expression.

The aunts would come on Sundays and tickle his chin, and jabber Da da da da. He would shake his head as if there were flies all over him, and if they kept it up he would snarl.

"Maybe he's a mute," Aunt Odette decided after a string of failures and he bit her. "This baby. But children always love me, every one of them."

She was fat and she had a big chest, like a pair of pillows; children must have gotten them mixed up.

"All I can think of is he might be a mute."

"That's a nice thought," my mother said. "Have to put him away in the Shelter. On second thought," she added, "at least if he's a mute he won't make such a racket."

"Oh mama!"

"What?" she asked me.

"You shouldn't, in front of him! He isn't deaf, anyway."

"He can't understand what I'm saying. Listen, wipe off the big platter and watch out you don't drop it."

That was her idea of conversation.

"Asshole mama."

Everybody turned around to see where that came from. It was Nicolas, saying his first words.

"Well how do you like that!" said Aunt Odette.

"Asshole mama, asshole aunt."

"That's a fine way to talk where'd you learn that!" mama said and she gave him a slap. It was his first. He didn't cry. He grinned. As far as where he learned it goes, I could have told them a thing or two. You can't be too careful around babies. I wiped my platter.

"Josyane taught him that," Chantal said. "At night she tells him all kinds of things. I hear her."

I put down the platter and jumped on her. The old lady

rushed to the aid of her child, the aunt tried to get hold of me, Nicolas bit Chantal on the calf and not just fooling around from the way she yelled, and then mama fell on her face, pulling the dishtowel down with her. We picked up the platter in pieces, I was tickled it was broken and not by me; all in all it was just another Sunday.

*　*　*　*　*

It was springtime again. There was a lilac bush in one of the last few gardens the Project hadn't swallowed up yet. I would see it on my way home from school, but I didn't mention it, the other girls would have made fun of me.

The only time I had to myself was when I went on errands. So I never kicked up a fuss about doing them; anyway nobody ever tried to take them over, it was such a habit now they didn't even think about it. I would dawdle along as much as I could without a bawling out, taking a little longer as the days stretched out later.

The 115 bus stops right in front of the Project, and all the people coming home from work pile off at the time I go marketing; I always see the same faces just about; I recognize them. We all recognize each other, but we don't show it; just think oh, I'm late today, or I'm early, or I'm right on time, depending on the load that pours out in front of the gate.

One afternoon, a man getting off the bus looked at me and smiled. He crossed the avenue toward the big apartments, and turned around to look at me. I wondered why that man smiled at me, because he happened to be one I had never seen before. It was strange and I thought about it later; anyway so few things ever happened to me that the tiniest detail would stick in my mind. I saw the man again, on other days, and each time he would look at me.

One day on my way home from shopping I came face to face with him. I was carrying two bottles of wine, a bottle of water, and the milk, plus the bread under my arm.

"That's a pretty heavy load for you, all that," he said as if we knew each other. "Want me to take it for you?"

"Oh, I'm practically home," I said. "I live right there."

"Too bad," he said. "I live over there," he added, and pointed to the big buildings. "For the time being. I see you a lot, carrying bundles. You have a lot of work?"

"Yes. Well, I go in here."

"Well, too bad," and he gave me back the bag. "See you soon, maybe?"

He crossed the avenue and waved.

I ran into him more often. I watched the buses, but he seemed to get home earlier, because I would meet him on the avenue; maybe he was waiting for me. We would walk together a little way; he'd take my shopping bag; sometimes we would go past the end of the Project, talking, and along the little street around the buildings to the gardens.

His name was Guido. He lived by himself. He talked to me as though I were a person, he told me about his life. He was away from home here, in his own country he had a house with a vineyard, and lots of brothers and sisters the way I did, very beautiful sisters who were getting married one after the other. We would walk a while, and he would leave me with his little wave and his smile. He was a very handsome man, dark with beautiful white teeth when he smiled, and blue eyes. He must have been at least thirty.

He was very lonely, and sad; the housing project gave him the blues. He told me that pretty soon the whole

[25]

world would be like that, and men who had anything in their gut would just have to take off for the planet Mars. He looked at me and said he was going crazy; but he smiled, he didn't look crazy at all, just the opposite.

"How old are you?" he asked me.

"Eleven." I was lying a little.

"Madonna," he said.

He told me he listened to his record player at night, it was an old beat-up thing but he loved music so much he'd rather have that than nothing at all; you have to have something you love in life or you're like an animal. I told him that if I didn't have Nicolas I would be like an animal myself, and that's when I realized it, it's crazy the things you discover by talking. I started telling him about Nicolas, and about how I thought he had a soul. He looked surprised. I explained what Mademoiselle Garret had said about them, and how I couldn't really believe everybody has one. He nodded.

"You're right, it is hard to believe," he said. "What about me, do I have a soul?"

He stopped walking so I could look at him; he was smiling, showing his beautiful white teeth. I told him I thought so.

"How can you tell?"

"I don't know. Just like that. I don't know. For one thing, you talk."

He would say, I get sick when I work on those houses; I don't know if I can keep on much longer. I think, You're the one who's building these houses, Guido, you who were born on the hills. Where he came from there was always sunshine, but there was no work. Some day though, he said, there won't even be hills left, God willing I'll be dead by then. I'm not built to stand that, I'm a man, not a robot.

"You must be right," he said, "that's why this is happening to me."

"What is happening to you?"

"How old are you?"

I had already told him, but he must have forgotten. I told him again.

"My God," he said.

He began to walk again. He took me by the hand. His hand was big and warm, it closed tight over mine. No one had ever taken me my the hand, and I felt like crying.

He told me that he had no wife, he couldn't go near a woman any more, they were as phony as the ads, he said, from seeing so many of them.

"You lose your soul fast here," he said. "And if you don't lose it you go insane. That's what's happening to me. With you," he added, smiling at me.

I hadn't told Nicolas about Guido in the beginning— a young man who got off the bus looked at me—it was too silly to talk about. So I told him that I had met a man from the planet Mars. He was practically invisible, other people couldn't see him, he was alone all the time. He didn't like it here, he thought it was ugly, but he couldn't get back home, he was lost. There was only one thing he liked in our world, the music. At night he would listen to it when he passed by the houses. Where he came from, everyone had a soul, everyone understood everyone else. Nobody talked to anyone here, people were locked up in their own skins and didn't notice a thing. He could smile at them all the time, or say hello, but they never answered; I was the only one. On his planet it was always sunny, and covered with vines, and the trees never lost their leaves; in the spring new ones came out, white ones, and they would turn green the next year, the trees looked like bouquets of flowers. What details I gave him about Mars, just to be able to talk about Guido one way or another. I made up the name Chow for him, because that was how he said good-by. We would wait till Chantal was snoring before we talked, even if she was only putting it on it kept her from hearing, and anyway she was scared stiff of Nicolas who never let her get away with things and who had sworn to kill her later on, when he was grown up.

School was over. It was summer. I met Guido every day, when he was through working; we went walking a little farther out, by the gardens. When I told him we were going away on vacation he turned gloomy. He would look at me, he would begin a sentence and not finish it, then set off again; we walked without talking, his hand squeezing mine, crushing it. My heart was heavy and I couldn't say anything either. Finally he asked me if I could get out earlier for the marketing the next day, Thursday; he would arrange to be free too; of course I could. We made a real appointment for a real time at an exact place, a little off from our own buildings, at the Montreuil road sign.

He had a scooter a friend had lent him; he asked if I'd like to take a ride with him. Would I! Ride on a scooter!

I was in seventh heaven. He still seemed gloomy, he drove fast and pulled all kinds of tricks, I had to hang on to him tight, it was terrific. We turned into the Bois. He took a little road, and stopped.

"Let's stretch our legs a little, you want to?" he said.

I jumped off the scooter. He leaned it against a tree.

"Nobody will steal it?"

"We won't go far. Just a little way. To tell you something."

We walked a short way along a path. He was holding my hand.

"So you leave tomorrow?"

"Yes," I answered sadly. I wasn't looking forward to it.

"You know . . ." he said.

"What?" I asked after a minute, when nothing seemed to be coming.

"Oh!" he said. He turned to me and gave me a wild look. He took my two hands and suddenly he fell onto his knees and pulled me against him, and he started to talk in Italian. What he said I don't know, I don't know Italian, but I know when I heard it, I never heard anything so beautiful, I understood all of it. When he kissed my face he was burning hot, his hands were burning where they touched me and from time to time he would look up at me and ask me a question, did I want to, did I want to, all he said in French was I don't want to hurt you, I swear, I swear, it's because I love you, and then he said again in Italian that he didn't want to do anything that would hurt me, I believed him, I let him, I didn't want to stop him, not at all and less and less, as his lips came closer, and when I felt the heat of them I wouldn't have stopped him for the whole world. It was good, it never ended, my back was against the tree, Guido was on his knees in front of me, I could hear the birds, I didn't know there was anything so good, and at the end there was a limit I had to moan Guido clutched me with all his might and he moaned too, my legs wouldn't hold me up any longer. He lay me down on the ground, or maybe I fell, I don't know, he looked happy, he was talking again and he started over, he said he would never stop, I understood Italian better and better. I would never have stopped either, when he let me go a little I would hold him, at the end I almost hurt, I could hardly stand it, but what a shame! I wanted it to go on forever.

"You're not mad at me?" he asked when we finally got back to the scooter again, it was sundown, I was already pretty late.

"Oh no!" I said. I meant it.

He kissed me. I said "I didn't know there was such a thing."

"My God," he said, "how good you were! I knew you would be, I was sure of it all along."

We started again one last time but after that I really couldn't any more. "Maḍonna I'm out of my head," Guido said. We went back home full speed and he really was crazy then, we nearly got killed twenty different times, and he was singing a song from his own country at the top of his lungs. He dropped me off a little before the Project. He said something with *morire* in it, and a sad smile, and then he said Chow, twisting around on the scooter before he turned into his street.

"Well where did you get to? What about the spaghetti, when is it supposed to get cooked?"

I brought it in with me. I had bought it on the way with Guido, and carted it around in the saddlebag.

"I went for a walk."

"This is no time to go for a walk, while I wait around for the marketing."

Usually when she starts I keep quiet. But this time I couldn't take it.

"Just when is it the right time? There's always something I have to do! You've got me running from morning till night and the others just goof off! Why don't you get Patrick to run a few errands, he has the right to fool around as much as he wants!"

Patrick just barely managed to tear his eyes away from the TV—the only thing that could bring him into the house—and yelled "It's different with me, I'm a man."

I burst out laughing.

"A man! You don't even know what that is!"

It was really a poor time to pull that on me, oh he sure picked it!

"Louse!"

The twins lifted their noses out of their geography book (what is a peninsula? a peninsula is a body of land surrounded on three sides by water) and snickered, noisily.

"You want me to straighten you out?" Patrick asked me, very tough.

"Blah blah blah, blah blah blah," said the twins.

"And you two fags . . ."

"Blah blah blah blah blah!"

"Shut up," said the head of the house, "I can't hear the program!"

"You're not missing much," said Patrick.

"Blah blah blah blah," the twins chanted softly. "Somebody's gonna get it again."

"You going to keep still?" mama said. "Your father's watching a show. Josyane, grate the cheese."

"Where'd you go on your walk?" that little louse Chantal asked, smelling out something interesting, she had a real instinct.

"With a girlfriend of mine."

"What's her name?"

"Fatima," I said, picking her name out of a hat, none of them knew her anyway.

"Nice friends you got," said Patrick, the moralist.

"Go to hell, you microbe."

"Oh Christ," said the old man. "You can't give us a minute's peace the whole goddam day, can you?"

"Well, Josyane? What about the gruyère?"

"Oh hell! Let Chantal do it, she never does a goddamn thing! I'm sick of being the maid around here!"

I was wild. I could have killed them. Including the dumb sucker on the show, who they were asking how many miles there were between Sparta and Lacedaemon and who was standing there like a bump on a log making a fool of himself in front of ten million other idiots.

"He won't get it," said the father to his Eldest Son.

"He looks like a real stupe," the Latter agreed.

Catherine began to giggle, the way she did whenever Patrick opened his yap, even if it was to say the dumbest thing in the world. The old lady was giving me hell over the cheese, but between her teeth because of papa and the program. Finally I told her shit. She was so unaccustomed to that kind of answer from me, usually it came from Patrick, that she stood there blinking with the ladle hanging out of her hand and her mouth open, while I took off for my room. Actually, the secret is to snap back at them a little, what can they do about it?

I wouldn't eat; in the first place I wasn't hungry anyway, and besides I didn't need them and their mess; I had something else to think about, and I hadn't had a chance to do that from the minute I set foot back in this hole, not for one second, they were so quick to jump all over me with their dumb-ass yapping.

[32]

Well, they'd won. My treasure was smashed to bits, I don't know where, just swamped in rage, I couldn't get hold of it again. They're like acid, those characters, where they walk the grass never grows again, like they taught us at school about Attila the King of the Huns.

It did no good at all to say "Guido, Guido. . . ." Nothing. Oh the bastards!

And to think I could have lived for a hundred years without even suspecting there was something else in life besides their lousy gruyère, their spaghetti and their Social Security! Oh the bastards.

"Jo?"

"Aren't you asleep?"

"I was waiting for you. What are they hollering about?"

"They're worrying about gruyère."

"What's gruyère?"

"Cheese."

"I don't like it."

"You're right. Anyhow it's not worth worrying over."

"No," Nicolas agreed. "They're a bunch of assholes. What did you do today? Don't tell me—you were with Chow. It shows."

"It shows?"

Good lord, maybe it did show, come to think of it. Lucky it didn't matter with them, they've all got crap in their eyes.

"What did you do?"

"We went to the woods."

"What did you do in the woods?"

"Uh—we picked flowers."

"Where are they?"

It wasn't always so easy with Nicolas. I had gotten him used to being told everything.

[33]

"They're gone. They're the kind of flowers that fly away when you pick them."

"Then why do people pick them?"

"Because it's pretty seeing them fly away. And after you're sorry they're gone."

"I want some too," said Nicolas.

I should have expected that.

I promised him some. Blessings on Nicolas, the forest had come back, he had brought it to me. It occurred to me that I was sure to be sad, and I would rather be sad from longing for something than from never even knowing it existed.

Chapter 3

So vacationtime came, no fault of its own. The plant closed for August. This time we weren't going off to our grandmother's place in Troyes to dig her garden and mend her rabbit hutches, and come back with blisters and backaches. We were going to a hotel in the country, like real people on vacation, and we would get a real rest, from morning till night, not doing a thing but breathing the fresh air and storing up health for the winter; we would leave on . . . go by way of . . . eat at. . . . In short, they managed to turn a pleasure into a damn nuisance. They were talking about it since Easter—the route, the hotel, the activities, the schedule. Because they finally had the buggy, and the head of the family was now a master mechanic, nothing he couldn't tell you about the battery, the differential, the pumps, his face under the hood all Saturday afternoon, the conquering sponge on Sunday morning, running a contest with Mauvin about whose was shinier. He'd never touch the kitchen sink but that paint job was another thing. And it was "here let me polish you up a touch," proud as a bug, "you could eat off it," a regular little housekeeper.

We finally took off, the whole bunch piled one on top of the other; to make sure everyone took advantage of the car and was fully aware the old man had one, nobody was sent off to the Colony this year, money no object, and that was a real pity, the only good vacations you ever take are other people's.

Papa drove like a slob; all the other jockeys on the road made sure he knew it, and I got the willies every time he tried to pass someone. It was an old front-wheel-drive Citroën, the one we had, he said it could beat anything because of its Road-Holding Capacity. It must have been true about the Road-Holding Capacity, otherwise with papa driving it wouldn't have stayed there long.

Everytime one of those lunatics stuck his ugly puss out of his rattletrap to call him an ass, his eldest would blush; he was ashamed of his father, and he was in a rage anyway because he wasn't allowed to lay a finger on the precious machine, that was one point papa wouldn't give in on.

Every twenty-five kilometers Patrick would ask to take the wheel, just for a little, and the old man said plain no.

"Shit, I could do at least as good as you," Patrick said,

humiliated once again because his father had just gotten slapped down by a fifteen-ton trailer truck.

"It was my right of way!" the old man declared, speeding triumphantly around a left-hand curve which he took in the opposite lane, thank god nobody was coming on that side.

"Anything that big always has the right of way," Patrick pointed out. "Besides he was coming from the right, and that was in a populated area."

"From the right, from the right, I'll show you right!" he said, dropping the wheel to take a swing at the rebel's face; mama clasped Chantal to her breast as she watched a plane tree move in, papa caught the wheel again in both hands just in time, the son missed getting his punch; he took advantage of the situation.

"From the right. This is the right side," he said, pointing to it. Actually Patrick had a point.

"I know what I'm doing," declared papa, who drew new authority from his grip on the wheel. For a minute or so we hit a hundred and ten in silence.

"Peepee," said Catherine.

"Oh no!" said papa.

"I have to," said Catherine, and she started to whine.

"You'll wait until we stop for gas."

"You know she can't wait," said mama plaintively. "She'll do in her pants."

"Ah nuts," papa said, stalling for time.

Or else it would be Chantal feeling sick to her stomach; she couldn't stand riding in the car, and finally they had to put her up front with mama, next to the window in case. Patrick was in the middle, between mama and papa. In the back I had Nicolas sitting on me and half of Catherine; the twins were jammed into the other corner, looking out at the passing scene and exchanging reactions in their own kind of Javanese they had made up so no one else would understand them. Whenever we stopped Nicolas would pick flowers and throw them into the air, to see if they would fly away. We would climb back into the car, where papa had stayed fidgeting around and looking at his watch.

"I'll never keep up my average with this bunch."

Patrick began to snicker loudly.

"Look, you, I'm gonna leave you off right here on the road," said papa. "I'll just leave you right here you'll see!"

He thought having to get out of his beautiful car was the supreme penalty.

"Okay," Patrick said. "I'd rather be an orphan than a corpse."

Since we hadn't started up yet he got his smack.

The old man had a soft spot for the eldest of his sons, the one who carried on his line, so to say; but when it came to the car he was another man, full of get-up-and-go, dynamic, authoritative—it showed a new side of him.

"Get out," he said, opening the right-hand door, behind which mama was just pulling Catherine's pants back up.

"Maurice . . ." mama said weakly.

"It'll teach him a lesson," said the head of the family. "The snotty kid. It'll teach him a lesson, there."

Patrick stood there having a great time at the side of the highway. Papa started the car, with some difficulty because he was stopped in a patch of sand. Right away mama began making trouble, she thought he had been too harsh and she wanted to go back. He didn't.

"I'm just fed up with that snotty kid, always criticizing what other people do."

Actually he was glad not to have him next door making

remarks about the lousy driving all the time. We noticed it too but at least we shut up about it. He was taking himself a little rest period. When he had enough he let himself weaken. "He's probably learned by now," he said, and he made a U-turn on the highway it's just as well Patrick didn't see. He told us the gear shift in a front-wheel-drive Citroën always made a grinding noise.

Patrick wasn't where we had left him. Stationed on opposite sides of the road, mama and papa scanned the scene. Nothing. Anxiety set in. They called, Paaatrick! Paaatrick! I told you, mama said, I told you you were being too tough. I knew it. Papa didn't answer. The twins and Nicolas and I had found a blackberry bush and we were climbing around in it.

"You couldn't help us look instead of fooling around there?" I offered the idea that he might have thrown himself into the river running nearby, but I didn't really believe it. Cathy began to hiccup. I said maybe we had the wrong spot after all; was that foundation there before, I didn't remember seeing it when we let him off. The twins said they were positive it wasn't, they had seen a transformer. We managed to get them to backtrack quite a stretch that way, and by the time they were finished they weren't sure of a thing. Papa decided to notify the police and the Missing Persons, if you could call Patrick that. And to go on. Mama said she would stay in the village until they found "the little one," as they were referring to him now. All the yokels in the place were interested in us, mama was surrounded by hens, there are hens wherever you go. Papa, conscious of his responsibilities, decided that he would take His Dear Ones to their destination first, you couldn't drag young children like that around the highways, espe-

cially the little girl in her condition, Cathy was having con-
vulsions, and he would come right back for The Search.
Everyone was worried about Patrick, "the Little Lost Boy."
Papa kept saying "I was too strict, he's so sensitive," the
men were talking about dragging the river.

We met him a little farther on at an overpass sitting on
the railing and eating apples.

"You sure make lousy time," he said scornfully when we
pulled up in front of him. "I've been waiting for you about
an hour."

"Where the hell did you get to?" papa said completely
knocked on his ass.

"I went right past you. It wasn't too tough. And it would
have been even easier if you weren't driving smack in the
middle of the road. I was just about ready to leave, I was
starting to get sick of waiting around."

"Now look, what kind of crap you trying to give us?"
papa yelled. "I'm going to leave you right there again, you
hear?"

"Maurice. . . ." begged his mother. "Come on, get in,"
she told Patrick, climbing out with her Chantal in her arms
as fast as she could to let him by. "Hurry up, your father's
already wasted enough time with you."

Patrick got in with dignity, looking at everything disdain-
fully.

"I was in a Cadillac," he said after a minute, though nobody asked him. "Now there's real springs," he added after
we crossed a cobblestone section.

"Still you could have waited for us," mama said. "You
knew we'd come back to get you. We wondered where you
got to."

[40]

"Josyane said you jumped into the river," Chantal snitched, on an off chance.

"I didn't really believe it," I said. "That would have been too good to be true."

"Patrick would never do us such a favor," the twins said.

But Patrick wasn't paying any attention to our jabbering; he was describing everything the Cadillac had that this car didn't.

"And the gears can't grind, even with the biggest boob driving," he remarked as papa shifted into third, "since they're automatic."

"Why didn't you stay there?" I said, fed up. "Why did you bother coming back to us poor slobs why didn't you stay there in your Cadillac?" Patrick ignored the interruption and went on about the buttons on the dashboard.

"Whyn't you stay there, whyn't you stay there," the twins began chanting, drowning him out.

"Oh shut up," said papa who was looking for his headlights, night was coming on, you couldn't see a thing.

"This is the bad time," his wife remarked in the mood for conversation. "It's not light and it's not dark—twilight."

"In the Cadillac," Patrick said, "the headlights go on automatically when it gets dark."

"Shut your mouth, with your Cadillac," papa said.

"Patrick is a big fat bore," said the twins, "Patrick is a big fat bore, Pa-tri-kizzabore, Pa-bore izza trick, bore is pattycake—"

"Will you shut up!" mama said. "Oh these brats!"

"Never a minute's peace! Even on vacation!"

"Don't even let us enjoy a trip!"

"And we have to drag them along!" sighed the father with his burden.

More sighs. "Why'd you make us?" came the little voice from Nicolas, who everybody thought was asleep.

They didn't answer. There were muffled snorts. It was us, united for a moment in sweet laughter. We did have something in common, after all. The parents.

It started to rain and we had a blowout. The old man remarked that our luck wasn't too bad, this was the first trouble and it was a pretty common one, he said as he worked the jack in the torrent. Patrick was holding the lantern.

"In the Cadillac," the twins said, "when a tire blows out another tire comes and gets right on the wheel all by itself."

Patrick stuck with us though. Nights he never was such a big shot.

We got there. We woke up the hotel. The owner had rented one of the rooms when we didn't show up, during the season you can't let the rooms go empty. We settled into two, to wait till someone left. The next day the vacation would begin. I expected to spend my time loving Nature. No.

* * * * *

There were the same people here that I saw all the time. The only difference was that it was a little more crowded in this small hotel than in Paris where at least everyone had a bed to himself; and that people talked to each other. As they said, you make friends easier on vacation. I don't know how it could be any other way, seeing as how we fell over each other's feet every minute, we ate together at one big table noon and night and during the day we would go to just about the same places. On top of that nobody had a thing to do from morning to evening, since that's just what they were there for, and there wasn't even a TV to fill the slack time like before meals, so they would buy each other drinks then and sit around talking; or between dinner and bedtime, because if you go to bed right after eating, as somebody always remarked at that point, it's bad for the digestion; so they would go out for a walk along the road to get a breath of air before turning in; it was healthy, they would say, makes you sleep better; like eating an apple, or drinking a glass of milk, someone would add, and the conversation would take off on how to get a good night's sleep.

As far as I was concerned, I had trouble sleeping in the same bed with my sisters, Catherine always with her damn nightmares, tossing around, and Chantal with her damn snoring; and I couldn't even shoot the bull with Nicolas, he was in the other sack with his brothers.

It was pretty around there, they said. There were woods and fields. It was a wet year, everything was green. The old-timers, the ones who got there before us, would tell us where we should go, what to see in the area. People went for walks; they'd go through the woods and come back over the fields; they would run into other people who had gone over the fields and were coming back through the woods. When it rained papa would play cards with a couple of other jerks who were on vacation too. The kids would play some dumb game. The women sat at the other end of the table talking about their guts.

"We're getting a good rest anyway. And besides there's air," they would say. "For the children."

I didn't remember lacking air back in the Project. Anyhow not to the point where it drove me so bats I had to go look for it someplace else.

I wished to hell there was some homework I had to do

over the vacation. Trees to plant in staggered rows along crossing paths. Fountains filling basins. Conjugations. The verb *s'ennuyer* is such a hard one—where do you put the *yi?*

I tried making some up, but it didn't work; homework has to be required, otherwise it's not homework it's entertainment and as entertainment homework is a drag.

"Take Nicolas for a walk, will you, so we won't have to trail him around with us."

Even Nicolas and I couldn't think of anything to talk about, I don't know why, because after all there was never so much going on in Paris either if you really thought about it. Maybe it was the air; they were always saying that, too, that Fresh Air tires people out.

"Why don't we go home?" Nicolas asked.

"Because we're on vacation."

"Anyway we're getting a rest," mama kept saying. She had picked up the habit of helping clean the vegetables for lunch, beans usually, with a chunk of meat. Sundays we had chicken. One of the men would order a good bottle, the owner would make a special trip to pick it up, and it would provide a topic of conversation right off, whether it was better than the one before or not, and what year it was, and which was the best year out of the last few, and whether this year would be a good one, judging by the amount of sunshine and rain; at times like that papa would display a knowledge of wine he never gave any hint of in the city, you'd think the fresh air was giving him an education. As a matter of fact the other men were wellsprings of information too; they were inexhaustible about everything, discussing all subjects with great authority, each one out to show the others he was no dope and that he knew a thing or two. Especially on cars, which they always got around to when they had taken care of everything else, and none of which had any secrets from them, the Aston with her touchy steering, the Jaguar and her bitch shock absorbers and the Alfa with her endless tuneups, the 220 SL now that was really a hunk of car but you had to go to Germany every time she lost a bolt, the Americans let's not even talk about them they're all a bunch of cows, and when you came right down to it the best of them all was still the sweet little French Car, there you had the most features wrapped up in the smallest package, and economical too, five liters the hundred in the 4CV and so practical with her motor in the back because you could stick the baggage in front.

"Yes but you get into an accident and you get hurt, at least with the motor in front there's some protection."

"Maybe you're protected but the motor isn't, and that way what hurts is the cost."

"Better hurt from a cost than a cast!"

Laughing.

"Look, when it's bad enough to smash up your motor chances are you'll get knocked around yourself at the same time so where's the advantage?"

"Stability."

"Oh please, as far as Stability, the old Citroën," my father said.

"I'm not talking about bad accidents of course because when that happens of course you're stuck but the little bumps well there with the 4CV you never got to do anything but hammer out the dents."

"If it comes to that, you can get banged up from behind too."

"Yes but then it's the other guy who's in the wrong and the insurance covers it."

"It covers it the other way too."

"Not in a collision if it's your fault."

"Insurance or no insurance, if you want to know what I think, I'll take a car that holds the road, like the Citroën." That was papa. "With the Citroën" papa said "you never have any headaches. It'll never flip over. Take the turns, you'll feel it sticking to the highway, and the faster you go the better it sticks."

"Yes but you know the gas that thing eats up? With my 2CV I burn up five liters every hundred. The trip here cost me let's see five times six wait that makes three hundred, no three thousand, I mean thirty francs. You got to admit that's cheap."

"Economy is fine but safety first," said papa. "Now me with my family I need to think about safety, and besides if I divide by the number wait a minute, that makes ten times six let's see, yes and divide by nine okay it didn't cost me any more."

"Well I think I beat you mine came to wait . . ."

"You're only five altogether, we make nine. Just figure it out. And besides where would I put them all, in a 4CV?"

"Under the hood!"

Laughing.

"And where would I put the bags?" papa said. "Huh? Where would I put them. See."

"We get seven into my 2CV, and the safety is just the same, it's got front-wheel drive too."

"Yeah, but how fast do you go?"

Pieuchet winced: that was his great shame with the 2CV, not going fast. He knew it and he couldn't do a thing about it. On the road everybody passed him right by, he would get where he was going with his nerves frazzled and have to sleep a whole day.

"Getting here took me, I mean if that little bastard hadn't lost us a good two hours, it would have taken me let's see . . ."

"It took me around seven hours. A little less."

"So it would have taken me about five and a half, if I could have kept up my average. That's not so bad, huh?"

He was forgetting the time it took us to change the tire, besides shaving something off the over-all count, but that won him the conversation race that was the main thing.

"Maybe," Pieuchet said, "but after all when you're on vacation you're not in such a rush. And in town I have the advantage."

"Not on Pickup!" put in Charnier, the one with the 4CV. "Not on Pickup! The 4CV is the fastest there. That's the one that gets away from the light a good length ahead of the rest of them!"

"Yes but after that, I move up," papa said. "And I pass."

"Yes, and on the turn, I pass you again! The 4CV gets around, it's light, easy to handle . . ."

"It's so light it flips over like a pancake. One little gust of wind and bingo. On the way here I saw two of them off the side of the road with their paws in the air," Pieuchet said.

"There's no reason to drive like a damn fool," Charnier said.

"One little wind, and bingo!" Pieuchet said, delighted.

"The 2CV's made of cardboard, lay a finger on it you make a hole, that's all it takes," Charnier said.

"Just try it. We'll see who makes a hole first."

"The Citroën, that's real solid," said papa. "A tank."

"You can't turn it," Charnier threw in.

"Sure it takes more than a little girl to handle it," papa said. "It's a real machine, it's no toy. A man's car. And it pulls. Even uphill."

"You can't beat the 4CV on hills."

"Except with a Citroën!"

"When it comes to that, a Rolls would pass you like a breeze."

"I'm not talking about the Rolls. A Rolls is a special case. That's the prestige car. In this country we prefer not to make the prestige car, and build lots of good little buggies that do what they're supposed to do. The proof of the pudding is that foreigners buy them instead of their own makes."

"Less. They're buying less of them. They got the idea, now they're starting to turn them out themselves."

"Wait, just wait! Wait till they try it! They might just come back to our Dauphines! Our Dauphines can stand up to anyone mark my words."

"Well sure, the Dauphine . . ."

"Well yes . . ."

"Too bad it costs so much . . ."

"Yes and for the price you don't get that much more room than in a 4CV and when you got a big family . . ."

"France never built a better car than the old Citroën. Twenty years ahead of the World Automotive Industry."

"That could be, but they're not making them any more."

"No use crying over the past."

"They still stand up."

"There's more and more of them going to junk now, pretty soon you won't find the parts."

"The universal joint. That's the weak spot."

"They should have brought it up to date a little and stuck to their old motor. The DS will never touch it."

"Nah. The DS has a lot of bugs."

"Real boats."

"Hard to handle."

"Parking it in town, can't be done."

"And does it eat."

"You can't turn it," Charnier said.

"It's comfortable though," Pieuchet conceded. "In the old one it was bad sitting in the back."

"A car's not a bed. It's a means of transportation. Look at the size of the DS, and it holds less than the old Citroën did. Nine in there and plenty of room."

"Come to think of it what are you going to do next year," Pieuchet said to Charnier, throwing a mischievous glance toward his lady, who was sitting with the other wives at the opposite end of the table with her pear-shaped belly holding her a little away from it.

"Especially if it's twins," papa added slyly.

All the men pivoted around, chuckling, toward the women, particularly at her who was recently fertilized.

"So what do you think, will it be twins?" papa asked, throwing up a bridge between the sexes.

"The doctor says maybe," said Madame Charnier, turning toward the progenitors a face that already had the horsey look and placid smile of the mother-to-be.

"Aah, it's no worse than having one," said mine, the voice of experience. "And that way you'll have five right off, it's useful."

"They're cute, twins," said the wife Pieuchet, touched.

"I'll miss her," said Charnier, "she was a good little

buggy, but if there are seven of us I'll have to give her up. I'll miss her. She was a good little buggy."

"When I had mine they were all peaches and cream, real pictures. And look at them now!"

You couldn't see them, they were outside slopping around in the brook tending to their tadpole farm.

"What will you get instead?"

"I don't know. I'm thinking about it. Maybe a 2CV."

"They lost them on me for six months, and when we got them back . . ." mama dropped her voice probably in order to confide the dark secret of the Substitution to her close friends; the heads bent together around her.

"Get yourself a Citroën, that's the best. In the end. Even if it is expensive for gas at least it doesn't cost much to buy it, and either way it comes out even. In the end. Believe me. Get a Citroën."

"Yes but it still depends on what you can find. It's old by now."

"Well yes sure. Got to know what you're doing," said papa.

"When I saw my little baby stark naked in the middle of those cakes of ice, I'm telling you I really screamed. My God they're going to kill her I said, it's the only way to save her the doctor said and he was right."

The feminine gazes turned toward Chantal at the window where she was playing with the little Pieuchet girl dressing a doll and undressing it and dressing it again and undressing it again and jabbering something stupid. Seeing she was the object of attention she smiled and started feeling around under the skirt again, saying gravely that the doll had made peepee in her pants and they had to change her again.

"That's like Catherine," my mother explained to the other hens. "Just imagine at her age she still does. Where is she anyway? Josyane, go find Catherine!"

"She must be in the barn," I said without budging, I had dug up some book and I was reading.

"That's like my little Daniel," said the Pieuchet woman, "still doing in bed at three and a half, no way to break him of it. Every morning we'd find him wet, every morning he'd get his spanking, and every night he'd do it again."

"You didn't bring him?"

"We lost him," said the mother with a huge sigh.

"Ohh," said the others.

"Leukemia. When he was six."

"Ahhh."

"You bring them into the world and then . . ." She moved her arms as if to say they get away from us.

"Ah, how right you are."

"That's a woman's lot."

"And why so much suffering, you wonder."

They observed a moment of silence, to meditate.

"Josyane did I tell you to go get Catherine or didn't I?"

The book was about an orphan who had gotten herself knocked up by a duke, and she found out it was her brother, at least that's what I understood, anyway that's what the duchess told her, and she fled into the forest with her precious burden, and some character came along, the duchess's gamekeeper who had only one arm, and I wanted to find out what he was going to do with it. Anyhow it was a big pest to go find Catherine, and start looking for her underpants which she had probably taken off, that was the scheme she had figured out to cover up when she made peepee in them, she would take them off and hide them somewhere. Then she would sit down in front of a doorway to dry herself off, and all the boys passing by would look. When I tried to get her away from there she would kick me. It was easier to find the underpants, because as soon as I got close to where they were she would start to yell; that was a good thing because otherwise mama would get mad, underpants are expensive.

"It's raining mama, she must have gone into the barn to get out of it."

"What lousy weather," said the pregnant one.

"No it's not raining," Chantal simpered, to bother me.

"That's right, it stopped," said one of the fathers, standing in the doorway with his hand stuck out.

"We'll be able to go for a walk then."

"I don't know if it's too smart," said papa who had gone all the way out and was staring at the sky with a critical eye. "It's going to start again any minute."

"We haven't had such good luck this week, a lot of rain. Last week it was better. We had plenty of good weather," said Pieuchet, who had arrived before us and liked to act luckier than everybody else.

"Plenty, plenty," Charnier said. "Don't go overboard. It rained."

"It rained a little."

"It rained quite a bit," said Charnier.

"Less than this week," Pieuchet said. "This week it hasn't stopped."

"Tuesday it was nice."

"Between cloudbursts."

"Between cloudbursts, a whole day," Charnier said. "It was a nice day."

"It rained in the afternoon," said Pieuchet; "we were at the quarries and we had to get under a cliff, I remember."

"A shower," said Charnier, "just a little shower, five minutes later it was dry. We were in the village I remember, we didn't even have time to finish our drink, the sun was back out."

"Last year was when it was nice!" Madame Pieuchet put in. "Remember? We were at Lancieux. What a beautiful summer that was!"

"At least it was no better in July this year. That's a consolation."

"Rotten summer."

"It's good for the crops," Charnier said.

"Not necessarily. Not for all of them. 'August rain, wine a shame.'"

"Ah."

"It's spring rain that's good for the crops. Not the summer kind."

That was papa talking. I wouldn't have thought he knew anything about that either.

"Look, there it goes again, see."

"Just a little sprinkle. It won't last. See it's not making bubbles when it hits. When rain doesn't make bubbles when it hits that shows it's only a passing shower."

"It looks like it's clearing a little over there, by the transformer."

"It may turn out all right."

"I told you."

The weather bureau was stationed under the awning, observing the cloud movement. They calculated the wind direction. East-southeast. That was good, it was sure to clear up.

"You know, what I'd like is find a good 203," Charnier said dreamily, with his nose to the sky. "Not too new, but good."

"Peugeot you got to hand it to them, that's good French car-making . . ."

"A hundred thousand before the first checkup . . ."

"And parts, practically for nothing."

"The only problem is the price. Even old."

"It's tough braking in fourth."

"Ah no, that's just rumors."

"She's got a Chassis."

"Oh no she hasn't got a Chassis."

"I'm telling you she has a Chassis."

"No she hasn't got a Chassis."

"Come on."

"Please."

"How about another one while we wait?"

They streamed back toward the 32.

"Well we're getting a good rest."

I wonder why they don't just give us some shot to make us sleep for the vacation, that would give us a better rest even and at least we wouldn't have the annoyance of noticing it. Now that would be a real vacation.

One day we went off to see the dam. The men went into ecstasies over the concrete, the amount it took to hold back all that water, and the labor, Charnier asked the guards if they were sure it was strong. I can't think of anything more dismal than a dam, except maybe a canal, we went to see one of those too. Every day they looked for something else to visit. The women knitted sweaters for the winter, which wasn't too far off now. After lunch, the men would tell dirty stories. In the end the gamekeeper took the poor orphan in, and informed her that she was the true heiress to the château, which the duchess-mother had taken over illegally by switching babies in the cradle, but the orphan had a mark on her chest which the gamekeeper finally discovered, actually she had misunderstood his intentions. The heiress married the young duke who it turned out wasn't her brother now, and they had a lot of little dukes. Finally they all began talking about going home. The conversation started up about jobs, everyone told what he did, they compared the advantages and disadvantages, things got a little livelier. Too bad it's over we were really starting to get into the swing, alas the best of things must end. Besides when you come right down to it it's nice to get back to your own little place. You're glad to get away but you're glad to get back too.

The next shipment arrived while we were loading up the bags. They were immediately informed about the customs of the place, what time the meals were, how to stay on the good side of the owner's wife, where to go, what to see; that way they felt more at home right away.

There was a little boy who had a disgusted look I liked. Too bad, we could have been bored together. When we left I told him "What a shitty place this is you'll see." Just to give him strength, no reason.

We took off; big farewells all around, they would miss each other, they were real pals; they handed addresses back and forth, they would have to see each other in Paris, not lose track. The joys of parting. Everyone was on the step to see us off, the folks were waving from the car windows. Patrick was way in the back seat, covered with black-and-blue marks, the kids from around there had paid him off all in one hunk just before he left, five against one; the twins were examining their tadpoles in a bottle; Chantal was showing off in the sweater mama had made her. We pulled out, jerking, and Patrick never opened his trap.

"Well that's that," papa said rolling along the highway. "Another one over."

"Ah yes," mama came back.

We rode on. We were quiet. We were going home. Vacation over. Happily I watched the trees file past. The closer we got to Paris the more my heart danced.

Guido was gone.

Chapter 4

THE BUSES I WAITED FOR! SO many buses. The people I watched get off those goddam buses. Long after I lost faith, I still had faith—otherwise what was I waiting for if I wasn't waiting for anything? They had put up a bench there; it must have been for my sake, to give me a little rest, discouragement wears you out. There were times I couldn't carry a single bottle any more. I couldn't carry them. They would have fallen right out of my hands.

I sat on the bench. I didn't believe any more. I longed. I longed, I longed, I longed.

It still felt like summer; nature was beautiful here; there were stars. I could see them when I leaned my head back. Out in the country I hadn't even thought about them.

I walked through the little street where I had gone with Guido. But that didn't do a thing for me. There was a hole beside me, where Guido should have been.

A few more shacks had been torn down, roads cut through, gardens wiped out. Places change fast here. With a bulldozer it's easy; one fine day it turns up and the next you don't recognize a thing.

I roamed around the big apartment buildings, where Guido used to live; they had put smooth lawns everywhere with fences around them so the kids couldn't trample them, they'd planted young trees inside bars too so the kids couldn't murder them; that way they had a Park Area whether they wanted it or not. What I wonder is why they don't stick the kids inside the fences instead and leave the trees in the open around them. The old man's shack was gone, with its vineyard—Guido had told me it was a vineyard—and there was a row of apple-green street lamps where it used to be.

The Workers' Residence sign was gone from the last building, there was no one singing Italian through the windows anymore, or guys naked to the waist shaving; they weren't on the balconies calling to the girls at six o'clock; there were diapers drying there instead. It was over. Guido was gone because the houses were finished that's all.

At night the windows would light up and inside there were only happy families, happy families, happy families. Going by you could see them beneath the ceiling bulbs, through the big windows, one happiness after another, all alike as twins, or a nightmare. The happinesses facing west could look out of their houses and see the happinesses that faced east as if they were seeing themselves in a mirror. Eating noodles from the co-op. Happinesses heaped one on top of the other, I could have figured out the volume in cubic feet or in yards or in barrels, since I was so crazy about doing problems.

The wind blew over the Avron plateau, it blew between the apartment buildings like in the Colorado canyons, which could never be such wilderness. Instead of coyotes at nightfall, speakers howled the word on how everyone could have white teeth and shining hair, how everyone could be beautiful, clean, healthy and happy.

Happiness kills me. I cried. I don't even know if it was Guido I cried for. Maybe after calling him a Martian so often I was ending up crying for the planet Mars and for everything I had put on it, that wasn't on this one. I would walk around between the buildings and I would cry.

Those buildings were really strange. I don't know where in the world you'd have to go to find something that strange. I'm positive that a desert is just nothing at all next to them.

"Chow is gone Nicolas. He went back to Mars. He had enough."

I cried in my bed at night. I cried all the time those days, I don't know what was the matter with me, maybe I was at that age.

Nicolas would hear me crying, he would get up and come over to comfort me.

"I'll kill Patrick. I'll kill everybody. Chow will come back."

"It's not only Chow. I've had it."

"I'll kill them all. I'll drop an atom bomb and I'll smash all the buildings. Don't cry. We'll go to Mars too. When I grow up you'll be my little sister."

"At least I've got you. You understand everything, you have a soul."

"I have a red soul. I can feel it at night, right here. It burns me."

Nicolas went away to the clinic. His skin tests came out positive. Why him? Why not Chantal, since she was the one who was always coughing? It wasn't fair.

"One thing though," mama remarked, "that'll make room for the baby, I was wondering how we would do it about the beds."

She was starting her eighth month. There was no money for a new bed, and hammocks are dangerous, we read in the paper how that little girl fell out of her hammock because her parents didn't have anything to buy a bed with. She fell out while her father was looking out the window at the lot where his car was standing because he didn't even have enough to put gas in it.

"And suppose by some chance Nicolas doesn't die you never can tell, what are you going to do when he comes back?" I hollered, in a rage.

"We'll see when that happens. We've got time to think about it."

"You're right, after all maybe the baby will be born dead like the other one," I said in a sweet voice, as I finished drying the plate. "No point getting into a sweat ahead of time."

She couldn't tell just how she was supposed to take that, she watched me out of the corner of her eye to make up her mind, but I put a dumb look on and picked up another plate, and she couldn't decide. When it came to children still inside her belly she was a little sensitive.

I was getting more and more mean. I missed Nicolas, and I was afraid he would die; those are always the ones. And I was pissed off that another baby was coming, I wondered what kind of halfwit this one was going to turn out, and how he would manage to get on my nerves, not to mention the diapers I could look forward to, because with all the progress they still haven't figured out how to make babies that don't crap.

The folks were pleased. Might as well be eight people as seven, really. They would be able to keep up the payments on the car. They wouldn't want to give it up for anything in the world, especially since the Mauvins had just bought themselves a newer one, and had a mixer and a fur rug besides.

"And this here is my refrigerator!" Paulette crowed in the co-op, tapping herself on the stomach for the benefit of the other hens.

We would need triplets at least if we were ever going to get a fridge. My mother gave her a dirty look; Paulette was five weeks ahead of her.

"And I'll keep on going till I get a washing machine!"

"We already have the washing machine," my mother got even. "A long time ago. I feel it's the most important thing in a home. For the laundry," she explained.

"My husband can't stand anything but the best," Paulette replied, undaunted. "We'd rather take our time and have something really good."

She was referring to our crappy old machine, which was always going wrong; it had pissed through her ceiling once.

Mama turned against fate like a coward. "If my next-to-last one wasn't born dead, and if I didn't have that miscarriage in the beginning that left me sick for months and besides I never really got over it, we'd have everything by this time and maybe even the Prize."

"Well me I had three born dead!" Paulette said. "And you can see I'm still here! And I'm good for a few more," she said with her big healthy laugh.

A young mother with just three children, who was only expecting her fourth in the spring, gazed at her seniors with admiration and dreamed of entering the Career.

"Don't worry, Madame Bon," the lady at the delicatessen counter told her, "it'll come little by little, before you know it."

Another pregnant one entered and joined the chorus. I retreated behind the crates. No room to stand in the store any more, mornings in the co-op it was a real blimp contest, that Project isn't a residence it's a stock farm. And they're touchy on top of it, just better not brush up against them, with their precious burdens, they could run right over people, and especially me at the time I came up to their stomachs, I couldn't see anything else in the landscape and any minute I might be flattened out between two bulges.

Paulette plowed a path for her own through the others and walked out full of dignity belly first with her refrigerator inside and behind that the washing machine pawing the ground waiting to be fertilized.

She had a boy. She made nothing but boys, and she was proud of it. She would provide the nation with a firing squad at least, all by herself; it's true the nation had paid for them in advance, it had the right to them. I hoped there would be a war in time to put all this material to use, they wouldn't be much good otherwise, seeing they were

[62]

all a bunch of dimwits. I imagined the day someone would tell all the sons Mauvin Forward March! and boom, there they are all flat on the battlefield, and they put a cross over them: here fell TV Mauvin, Jalopy Mauvin, Refrigerator Mauvin, Electric-mixer Mauvin, Washing-machine Mauvin, Carpet Mauvin, Pressure-cooker Mauvin, and with the pension they could still buy themselves a vacuum cleaner and a family vault.

We had a girl. We split right down the middle even now, girls and boys. They called her Martine, in memory of that bonehead Martine Pieuchet from vacation who spent her life undressing dolls and making them pee through a little hole. The kid looked normal. I'd have to wait and see. I told myself that with a little luck in ten years she might be able to take over for me. I handed mama back the house with pleasure. When she wasn't there they acted like lords of the manor with their demands. Papa wanted his soup strained and a pleat in his pants. I don't know why he wanted a pleat in his pants just while his wife was in having a baby. He didn't run around, papa; at most he might hang around a little longer over his aperitif when she wasn't there; but never too much; he didn't drink either, at least not like some, certain exceptions, they're known for it in the Project; papa when he had one too many he was just a little thicker than usual, it didn't show; even when his wife wasn't home and he let himself go a little more, feeling freer naturally, he didn't hit us any more than before. Just he felt like the boss; with her he held back a little because she would right away point out that with what he earned, and the life she led with us, and her health, and she would start counting off such a rosary that he never felt like starting up again.

The minute she got home Chantal got sick—said she had a sore throat for the past week and that I hadn't taken care of her; it was true, every time I made her grate cheese she had a sore throat; I put cheese in everything, and I never cooked anything but stuff they didn't like, you get your kicks any way you can. So they were always very glad when mama came home with the new baby in her arms.

It turned out she was right not to get into a sweat, everything always works out, the bed problem solved itself: when Nicolas came back from the clinic Catherine was in the Shelter. They had to put her there, the school didn't want to keep her, she never caught on to anything, and she would keep doing all kinds of dumb-ass things that disturbed the classes; besides that they had discovered that she was half deaf, it wasn't only that she didn't understand anything, she didn't even hear it. They gave her some tests, the lady doctor from the Subsidies examined her for a half hour and said she had a mental age of four years, that it would be very expensive to catch her up, it was a long difficult treatment they couldn't take on, and even so the kid would never be able to earn her own living, and that the only thing to do was just put her in some good Asylum where nobody would ever have to worry about her again. Next case.

"That's a good setup they have there, though," mama said, "they fix you up in no time flat."

It seems that in the course of her morning that doctor had sent four of them off to the junk heap like that.

Both the parents drove her down there. They kept it a secret from her where she was going, for once the word Shelter wasn't mentioned, and the whole thing was treated as a pleasure trip. But Patrick decided it would be fun to let the cat out of the bag just when they were starting out, and that turned it into a real hell. Catherine was torn away from the furniture piece by piece and dragged to the car practically on her stomach howling. The ladies came to the doorways outraged, one of them yelled something about calling the police. They wouldn't stand for anybody touching a hair of someone else's child; that was one thing, there were very few Child Martyrs in the Project. With those walls you could hear everything through, it wasn't long before any child-beater was spotted and reported, the Social Worker would move into action, and order would be restored very quickly. And if it wasn't in the Project it was at the school, the teachers were on the lookout for them; once there was a little girl martyr in our class, the teacher tried to give her a hard time, the kid didn't dare say a word; she was covered with black and blue marks. Finally they got her to tell, her picture was in the paper, and she went right off to the Welfare. Kids really do have more protection nowadays.

Anyway in our case the Social Worker showed up to help the parents out, and the ladies realized that everything was in order. Catherine howled that she didn't want to go to the Shelter, she had yelled so much that she hardly had any voice left, and held on so hard she had hardly any strength left; she may have been crazy but she knew what was good for her. She was still hanging onto the bumpers. But now it was three against one. They jammed her inside, I saw her ugly face one last time, the kid was sure no beauty, all puffy and smudged with grease and tears. She tried to climb out the window, they rolled up the glass. She found the strength to yell once more before it closed. The innocent was calling her brother. The car went into gear, started off, disappeared. I began to cry. A yard away from me I saw Patrick, with his head high; he turned away from the gate and went off whistling, with his hands in his pockets. I threw myself onto him so fast he never saw anything coming, and in the same lunge I landed him a tremendous punch in the jaw. It came from a long way off that one. He pulled himself together, the twins went for him in the belly; Chantal saw her chance and pinched me. I sent her rolling with a good kick. The watchman came running to pull us apart.

"If that isn't terrible," one of the ladies said, "the minute the parents turn their back."

"Shit on you," I answered her, "it's none of your business."

"Go fuck yourself," Patrick told her, and he had a point.

His mouth was bleeding; I had broken one of his teeth don't ask me how, some miracle. The hole stayed and it always did me good to see it. After all it was the only thing we had to remind us of Catherine.

There was a family conference that night after the watchman's report and a survey of clothes damage—something they always took very hard. The mending would be my job in any case.

"We work our fingers to the bone for that little bitch and all we get from her is trouble."

"That goon there is the one who told Cathy she was going to the Shelter," the twins said.

"You," Patrick said, "you two just better keep your traps shut and say thanks when you get a little food in your plate." He was lisping because of his tooth. "You're not even our blood," he said.

"You can shove your blood right up your ass," the twins said, and the one that was closer to papa got a smack but it didn't bother him, those twins were tough.

"You can eat it for salad," said the other one who was farther away from papa, "it's blood from a turnip," and he got his from mama who unfortunately was next to him.

Then the parents exchanged a long look. I knew the story. From certain references as broad as a house that they let drop from time to time, thinking we were too dumb to catch on, I gathered that they had started some kind of investigation about a Child-substitution, like all the examples in the newspapers, which had given them the push. They wanted to get back their beautiful babies, all peaches and cream the way mama saw them now in her memory, God knows what they were really like, if it was me I'd watch out, I'd hold onto these two who at least weren't cretins, that's already something. But everybody called them Arabs and that killed the parents, all the more because it really might be the truth. They did get along awfully well with the Arab kids, for that reason and also because they wanted to bug Patrick's gang who were always fighting with them. That made trouble with the other families, our parents finally got embarrassed, they were sick of those twins, they would have liked to get some others.

The kids realized something was up themselves, they weren't deaf. They kept to themselves more and more, and they were turning sullen.

In spite of the slaps they were breaking up at the sight of Patrick, whose lip happened to be bleeding at the moment thanks to me, and leaking the precious Rouvier blood.

"Boy are you handsome ugly puss you got no teeth you're cross-eyed . . ."

[67]

Patrick began to get up with his big-shot look; papa sat him down again with a firm and gentle hand.

"Let them alone," he said with contempt for such as were already gone from this world. I knew the whole question was finding the real ones before letting these two go, to keep the number up, and if the others were dead that would be a drag. "And you two shut up!" papa added in a rougher voice for the twins. "Just don't be too smart, take my advice."

They kept quiet. They smelled the wind. There was total silence, something that never happens in our house; instinctively we all looked around the room, what was it that was missing? Catherine. Whenever there was some kind of scene we used to hear her imbecile laugh, and it was gone. It left a vacuum. With no particular expression to my voice, I said "Silence is golden."

Mama went to get the noodles, everyone held out his plate. I said "What's it like, that Shelter?"

They made some vague noises, shrugged their shoulders, and papa swiveled around to turn on the TV which he had forgotten to do in the heat of action; the picture jiggled around, he couldn't manage to tune it in. I said "Maybe she won't live . . ."

Not a word from any of them. Papa twiddled the knobs. Silence again. I said "That would be the best thing for her."

"Goddam it," said papa, "what's wrong with this thing?"

"The tuner," Patrick said. "You got to push it farther."

"Who wants some more noodles," mama said. "Chantal, you aren't eating?"

"I'm not hungry," Chantal said. "It hurts here," she said, pointing to her chest and starting to hack; she said

I kicked her in the lungs. But I knew I caught her in the gut.

When she finished her coughing fit, I said "If Catherine died, would they stop her Subsidy?"

"Now that's enough!" papa said, and banged his hand on the table. "Mind your own business!"

He turned the TV up full blast.

Nicolas went into Catherine's bed. Life goes on.

Spring came. Summer. Then winter.

I got my diploma the first try; lousy luck; I would have liked to stretch it out another year, but they passed me. I wouldn't be able to go to school any more.

At Guidance they asked me what I wanted to do in life.

In life. Did they think I knew what I wanted to do in life?

"Well?" the lady asked.

"I don't know."

"Well, let's see—suppose you had your pick."

The lady was nice, she asked her questions gently, not like a teacher. If I had my pick. I shrugged my shoulders. I didn't know.

"I don't know."

"You never asked yourself that question?"

No. I never asked it. At least never with the idea that it called for an answer; anyway it wasn't worth the trouble.

They made me string beads with three holes onto three-pointed needles, put things together from pieces, work my way out of a maze with a pencil, find animals in ink blots. I never saw any. They had me draw something. I drew a tree.

"You like the country?"

I told them I didn't know, I thought probably not.

"You like the city better?"

To tell the truth I don't think I liked the city any better. The lady started to get annoyed. She suggested a whole bunch of different kinds of work and every one was as boring as the next. I couldn't choose. I didn't see why you had to knock yourself out ahead of time deciding how you were going to sweat. People did whatever job they managed to get hold of, and anyway every job was a matter of going somewhere in the morning and staying there until night-time. If I had any preference at all it would have been for something where you had to spend less time, but there weren't any like that.

"Well," she said, "there's nothing that appeals to you especially?"

I thought for awhile, but nothing appealed to me.

"But you did so well on the tests. Don't you feel any kind of vocation?"

Vocation. I opened my eyes at that. In one of those books I had read the story of a girl who had a vocation to go take care of lepers. I didn't feel any more urge to do that than to work in some factory.

"Anyway," my mother said, "it doesn't matter if she doesn't want to do anything, she's more use to me in the house than outside it. Especially with two extra. . . ."

They thought it was twins this time.

What I missed right away was school. Not so much the classes themselves, but the walk there and above all the homework at night. Maybe I should have told the counsellor that I liked to do homework, maybe there was a job where you do homework all your life. Somewhere, I don't know. Somewhere.

I felt as if I had nothing to do. I didn't have a minute free but I felt as if I had nothing to do all the time. I would try to think what I could have forgotten, where, when, what? . . . I don't know. Instead of hurrying to get through, I would drag things out; get through for what? At night I was exhausted, my eyes would close, it seemed to me there wasn't enough light, or that there was too much of it. I don't know. Before, at night, I used to begin to wake up, now I would practically fall down. And once I got to bed I couldn't sleep. I would shed a few tears. It had become a habit. I didn't even know what to think about.

Winter went by. Spring came back again. Spring, spring. . . .

Chapter 5

The italians were at Sar-
celles. They were building new houses. Liliane Bourguin
told me. Her sister had just gotten married, they had found
an apartment over there, there were some, and Liliane went
over. She heard about the workmen. It was the big story
around there. They lived there while the construction was
going on, in dormitories. Daytimes, when the husbands
left, they would go up to the women who would call to
them from the windows. Anyway that's what people said.

It got me all of a sudden. My memory came back. And

in a funny way; it was what I had forgotten the most completely that came back. Now I didn't remember anything
else but that: the woods, what Guido did to me in the
woods. I didn't understand how I could have forgotten
such a thing. I must have fallen on my head. I wondered
why I had gone looking for crazy explanations and stories
about Martians and all, when it was so simple, just that
Guido was a man and that was enough, a man, handsome,
with beautiful teeth, and not some "invisible smile" and
God knows what all, and what I wanted was for him to do
it again, what I wanted was the thing itself, plain and
simple, it was as if I had made up that whole big story just
to hide that from myself. How stupid you can be when
you're a kid. I began to suffer, and this time I knew exactly
what I missed. No more of that vague stuff, reveries of
beautiful dusks against a setting of cement, or melancholy
about a hard world, it was clear as spring water, so clear
that it hurt my belly, all the more since it had been sensitive
for a while now because of the age I was.

So the whole thing was how to get over there, and it
wasn't easy at all; it was in another suburb, it would mean
taking the bus to the Porte des Lilas, the PC to the Porte
Saint-Denis or Pantin or La Villette, or else the métro and
change twice, and then I don't know, or else the métro as
far as the Gare du Nord and a train from there to I don't
know where, from what Liliane said it was in some out of
the way place, anyhow it would take a whole afternoon just
to go and come back. I could have managed to scrape up
the cash for the tickets, but what about the time? I didn't
have the time. I didn't see how I could make it. Not that
they checked up on me. But the household practically de-

pended on me and if I let it go as much as an hour it was sure to fall apart and there would be big trouble.

Besides all that I wasn't even counting the time it would take to look for Guido like a needle in a haystack in the midst of a place with fifty thousand inhabitants. I knew what developments were like; our Project had about two thousand in it, and the joint across the way had just about double that; they gave me some idea what fifty thousand was like. I could wander around inside for a hundred days and a hundred nights howling at the moon not only without spotting one Italian but without ever even finding my way back out.

That was the only thing in my head now, and I could see Guido as if it had been the day before, with his white teeth, and my sack full of bottles in my hand, and the scooter leaning against the tree that day, and every detail of what happened next, I could see Guido shining like a lamp in the midst of all those fifty thousand fatheads over there, and myself heading straight for him on the first try and him saying Here I am, take me away please please please! I twisted around in my bed but I never got the same result even doing it to myself and that got me nowhere. The only solution was to go there.

What I really needed was a scooter. With a scooter I could get there fast, I wouldn't lose any time. First I thought of swiping one from the parking lot; all I'd have to do was watch for when they left them and when they came back for them. But first I'd have to learn how to use one.

I watched the boys playing around at the gate evenings after six, stepping on the gas, gunning their motors, shoot off, come back, circle around. Those things were damn useful. Some of them had regular scooters, others had little motorcycles, red, or blue, the dumb ones had fringes on them. I could do without fringes, as long as it moved. I would watch them take off along the avenue, three or four of them, sometimes with girls on the back. I would die of longing; for the scooters I mean; I would practically devour them with my eyes. Of course those idiots thought it was them I was interested in, they would drive circles around me to show me what big shots they were. I would be watching the wheels, and their feet to see how they worked them.

"Didi has eyes for you," Liliane informed me; she was a year older than I was, so she knew more about it.

"Me?"

"Oh don't act so surprised! After all you got a pretty little puss in your own way, as if you didn't know it."

She was what they might call a pretty girl: hair falling down her back like Niagara, reddish, and she wore make-up base and wide belts.

"If you just did something with your hair."

She grabbed a fistful of my hair and pulled it up like a movie star. "Look."

I couldn't see, we were down in the courtyard and there was no mirror.

"You don't need a mirror, dope, just look at the characters going by."

She was right, there was one who turned around laughing fit to kill. But he must have been a family man and besides he was on foot.

"I don't care about that stuff," I said scornfully. "The only thing I'm interested in is scooters."

But still I did my hair the way Liliane said, it was some progress anyway, why spit on progress? It was no pain seeing guys turn around when I went by. Why deprive yourself of a few kicks on the pretext of having a big scheme in the back of your mind.

That was how I finally got next to the scooters. And when I was real close, nobody objected to letting me climb up on the back. I asked questions about how it worked. I got a reputation for being interested in mechanics, which for a girl did me good.

The boys had two arms two legs and a head too. That made them passable. Too bad they talked. But anyhow when the scooter was moving you couldn't hear them. All I wanted was for someone to teach me to drive. Didi was the most willing, because he really did have eyes for me, as Liliane had noticed. All I hoped was that I would get to drive before the houses were finished over there. I wasn't so dumb that I didn't know that actually I would have gotten there faster just cutting out for a day on the public transportation, and putting up with a bawling out when I got back; but I had the scooter on the brain now and that's the way it was, the two things went together now, we all have our own little ways and that one must have suited me I guess, since I stuck to it.

At night we would go to a movie. As soon as the dishes were done the folks would let me go, they even gave me the dough for it, they were nice when it came to that, movies were something they could understand. After all I had no more homework to do, I had to fill my time somehow, and I've got to admit movies were a good substitute for homework. I could have gone every night, and there wasn't a single picture I didn't like; all it took was something happening on the screen with no interruption. I was always sitting with Didi, and he would feel me up. All the guys had a girl they would feel up. I was the youngest, and the newest one on the scene; Didi was just a kid, he was fifteen, I hardly felt it.

Guido had whiskers; his face prickled; it was a completely different thing.

Didi was no bother while I watched the movie; just the opposite, the two things mixed, they went together; lots of times I would forget who it was; he would slide his hand under my sweater, which I wore with nothing underneath. Liliane wore bras, she had a big chest.

"Jo has nothing on underneath," Didier said. "It's a lot better."

"Let's see," Joël said, like he was kidding.

Didier wanted to show he was broad-minded, he said "By all means." Liliane was sitting on the other side of Joël. She leaned forward, she hadn't followed the conversation too well, and Joël hadn't tried too hard to keep her up on it. It was the intermission. Joël bought Eskimo pies for everybody. When the lights went out again, I felt Joël's hand sliding under my sweater too, from the left. The two boys touched hands, they smothered a laugh. I completely missed the credits and the first shots; that time it really did something to me, I started to think there might be something to hope for even from boys.

Joël watched me from that night on. He would stare at my sweater. Joël was nineteen; that was a step up anyway. Bit by bit, slowly, and by pretty roundabout paths I admit, I was getting closer to Guido.

"Sunday we're going for a ride," Joël told me. "If you want to come just be at the gate at two o'clock."

It was the whole crowd of the big kids, five six boys, I had seen them lots of times taking off after lunch on

Sunday, with girls; this was the first time they asked me; I was growing up.

Joël had taken the opportunity to ask me when he was alone and so was I. But it was Didi who took me on his scooter as usual. I went on condition that he would teach me to drive it. I wasn't losing sight of my plan.

I learned to dance that day too. They all showed me; Joël squeezed me the tightest. We were drinking wine.

At a moment when we were on a part of the dance floor away from the others, Joël grabbed me by the hand and pulled me outside, to his scooter. Before I got on I asked him "We're coming back though, aren't we?"

"Don't worry," he said, "it's okay with Didi."

"Not because of Didi, because I want to learn to drive the scooter."

"You'll learn," Joël assured me, "you don't have to worry any about that, you'll learn."

Satisfied, I climbed up behind him.

I knew what he wanted. At least to begin with. As soon as we were lying under the trees in a quiet place he pulled up my sweater. He had been wanting to do that for a week, and it was pretty much agreed. He looked at my breasts, he stroked them and kissed them, and he gave me a whole lot of compliments, how they were a change from Liliane's, hers were too big. When he started on my skirt I hoped for a minute that he was going to do what Guido did and because of that I let him take everything off me without putting up the least little resistance. But he lay right down on top of me. I hesitated a second. I really didn't have much of an opinion and in the time it took me to decide on one it was practically too late and then wow.

"Quit yelling," he said, "somebody might hear you."

That was reasonable and I shut up. Besides it didn't hurt that much. For one thing it was a lot quicker than I I would have expected, I hardly had the time to think about what I was doing before it was over, he was standing up and buttoning his bluejeans.

"Okay let's go."

I put a cheerful face on. I didn't want to look like some boob. The scooter didn't feel so good. On the way back Joël told me "You're a good kid."

Evidently the others hadn't even noticed we were gone. At night we ate hot dogs and French fries and drank more wine; I learned to shoot a rifle too, and Joël bought us brandies; he was the one with the most cash. And I think he was in a good mood. Me too. I was feeling pretty good, at least there was some action in my life and it was nice, we were having a good time. It was a change anyway.

I wasn't in such hot shape for learning to drive the scooter, but Didi didn't think of offering again. We tore into the woods at top speed. We turned down a path and ended up in a clearing. They seemed to know the place well. They cut the motors and switched out the headlights. We got off. I was with Didi, it seemed to be sort of taken for granted now. I didn't make any fuss either, it wasn't worth it now. And it felt good to have a boy on top of me, the only trouble is that it's over so fast. But that's life.

Afterwards Joël came back. I don't know where Didi got to, and I didn't much care. I could hear the others not far off; it was dark, it was nice, we felt good. Joël told me I was really nice. He stayed with me. I came back home on his scooter. I saw that Pascale was on Didi's, he was doing okay. I wondered whether Liliane was going to be mad at me, but she was with Bob and they were pasted together kissing. Everyone looked very happy, I don't see why I shouldn't have been. It was a good day. I didn't learn to drive but that wasn't worrying me. It wouldn't be long before I did, that was for sure.

I was the first one home. The parents were in the country with the small fry, at our aunt's house. Patrick came in a little after me. I was taking a bath; Liliane had told me how to do it, not realizing how soon I'd be following her advice; or maybe she did. I heard Patrick moving around and getting into bed. I was in bed myself when the rest of them got back, they had been stuck in traffic for an hour and a half, but I wasn't sleeping. I had a little fever, and it was burning me up. I couldn't get to sleep.

When Chantal started to snore, Nicolas got up and came over to my bed.

"Don't you feel good?"

"Sure I do . . ."

"I heard you moving around, you're breathing hard."

"No, no, everything's fine. I had a little wine."

"Where were you?"

"Dancing, out at a place on the Marne."

"You went with the boys?" he asked.

I don't know if he meant what I meant when I said that. Anyway, what could I answer? "Yes."

He shook his head. "I'm too little," he said. "If I was big you wouldn't go with the boys," and he went back to his bed without kissing me.

* * * * *

Really, the great thing about it isn't so much what it feels like during, it's that it leaves you wanting to do it again. I had something to think about, instead of nothing.

Days I would think about the night, and during the week I would think about Sunday. That fills up a life.

"Well Josyane, dreaming?" mama would say when I did something wrong, which happened often.

And how, I was dreaming. If she only knew what about. At the time I was busy teaching Didi, he was the most likely one to give me what I wanted, which was something very particular. It gave me quite a special feeling to walk through the little streets looking for a good dark spot, my underpants stashed in my bag ahead of time, imagining the moment when I would have the boy there on his knees in front of me, in the shadow; oh he was no match for Guido, Guido did it on his own, by inclination, you could tell he loved it, and this one only did it because I made it a condition; but I got along; and what was terrific was standing there in the shadow with my head free and my back leaning hard against the wall, looking at the sky, seeing nothing but the stars when they were out, alone, really, and down below very far off way down there the boy more and more forgotten as the feeling comes and climbs as if it came right out of the ground. That was it, that was what made me flip. After I would let him make love fast. That was what he wanted, those three little minutes to comfort himself. They're strange.

"Josyane what the hell are you doing! look at all those wrinkles you're ironing in!"

"Just do it yourself if it's not good enough," and I quit. She would never sock me now, no more than she would hit Patrick, he had told her "That's the last one, I warn you, next time I give it back and you won't come out on top I'm warning you." She took him at his word and didn't try it again. What could she do? We were too big for her. And there were a lot of us: six against one, not even counting Martine who had started to crawl and little Pascal who had turned out not to be twins, just one baby, and didn't have teeth yet but he would grow up someday too, and become a threat. Papa butted into our battles less and less too, he was tired at night when he came home after a hard day's work, but actually it was a way of getting out of it and we knew it. They were outclassed by their eggs, they should have thought of that before they laid so many, you have to take the consequences. They don't look ahead enough. When children get to be a certain age parents should ask for a pistol permit, and set up a militia. Everybody was in the same boat in the Project, just because they didn't take steps in time, and why should we look out for them, said Nicolas, who wasn't the least dangerous by then far from it and some of the others had a few ideas themselves like putting ink into the old man's wine, as Nicolas said either don't have us at all, or else tell us why.

So nobody asked Patrick to account for what he did when he went out, until the day the cops would take over directly, they're organized for it, and equipped; meanwhile during that interim period the parents had the feeling it wasn't their business any more, and it wasn't; as for me I did what I wanted with nobody giving a hoot, like the other girls, except Ethel who was proper; but the Lefranc family was a different type from ours, there were six or seven like that in the Project, everybody knew about them. The Lefranc father would go from door to door with his petitions in hand, never getting discouraged, and anyway practically everybody would sign them usually, why should he complain? "You must be for peace, certainly," he would say, and of course everybody was for peace, how could they be against it? and papa would sign the petition and go down to wash the car, and Lefranc would knock at the next door. "People like that, they're sort of like priests," papa would say, feeling a little sorry for him. Every Sunday morning you'd see Frederick, the oldest son, selling the *Humanité-Dimanche* in the market place, with three four pals, yelling very loud in the middle of all those hens going by paying no attention to them. I would talk sometimes with Ethel. I envied her, because she was still going to school, a school in Paris; she was studying to be a teacher; she liked it. She told me it was hard, there was a huge amount of homework, sometimes she had to work till after midnight, my dream. But in her house it was the mother herself who took care of the kids, besides they only had four and now that Ethel was studying they let her completely alone about the housework, she couldn't have handled it. I would have liked to be in her shoes; but being a teacher wouldn't tempt me, because of the kids. I don't like kids. We had an argument about that, she thought I was wrong, that you really had to form kids and they could be terrific; most of the kids here weren't formed, they let them run around and didn't spend any time bringing them up right, I said how could they they aren't themselves they don't know a thing and they don't give a damn; she agreed with that. She said Why don't you come with us on Sundays, instead of hanging around with that crowd? There was something a little scornful in her voice when she said that, and it put me off— what business was it of hers? When it came to that subject we didn't get along; she would try to preach to me, but it didn't go. Ethel was more intelligent than me about a lot of things, but the truth was that I knew more than she did on that point and as smart as she was, next to me she was just a kid.

You could see it, too, just by the way she acted, and the way she walked, like a good girl, without looking around, always thinking to herself. I used to be like that before; now I would march right down the middle of the walks, and I would look people in the face, I had the devil in my flesh then; I would have grabbed everyone, even family men. But with a couple of exceptions they were satisfied just to give me little sneaky glances and go on their way back toward mommy and grub and yapping kids, it would break me up because I knew what they were thinking, I was beginning to know men. They were just too chicken to do what they really wanted.

I say with exceptions because there was one exception, René. He had a livelier stare than the others, and more insistent, that's the whole thing right there, instead of turning away it would stick, so that after a little while he was dying for it you could see it all over him, and I wasn't surprised when he came up to me. He started by talking to me in a stern tone of voice, or anyway pretending to, testing the ground, telling me I shouldn't look at men that way. Or accidents can happen, he threatened, when he saw I didn't look as if I was about to apologize; I was grinning. And just in case I didn't know what he meant, he added with more and more of a glint in his eyes, he was ready to show me, and while he talked he was looking all around as if he was hunting a place for it and then I really started laughing because that was the end, looking for a secluded spot around here, that was insanity, inside or outside here you're naked as a goldfish and within the sight of someone you can't see, especially since most of them have binoculars. So anyhow one Saturday afternoon he told his wife he was going to the *Bazar* to buy some tools and next thing, we were walking through the Vincennes woods looking for that secluded nook away from inquisitive eyes, which he seemed particularly worried about since I was a minor. Of the two of us he was the one who had the shakes the most, but his desire was stronger than his fear, he would squeeze me from behind, catching me every now and then and holding me against him to show me what it was doing to him.

"You make me so goddam hot, that's why," he said. "You're driving me nuts, you know it. Look, feel this."

He wasn't kidding. Finally we found a place, with nice grass. I love grass. He had big broad hands that took hold of everything at once.

"How fresh! Fresh as a rosebud! Oh hell. You asked for it."

I thought he was going to crush me. I couldn't move, I was nailed down, he was on me with his whole weight and rammed all the way in.

"When I think how I have a daughter your age, when I think how I have a daughter your age," he kept repeating, "when I think how I have a daughter your age," and it didn't seem to slow him down one bit.

I must say it gave me a real bang, more than with the boys. Maybe because he was heavier. Or because I was proud to have a real man. No two ways about it, boys are still very feeble, very light. You really feel it with a man. It left me all weak.

"When I think how I've got a daughter your age," he said again afterwards, when we were dressed again and ready to go back. But not in the same tone as before. He looked at me and shook his head gloomily.

"It's awful. . . ." he even added.

Shit!

We got back to the road. I could have started all over. That was probably the trouble with men, compared with boys, they don't start right in again. He was in a hurry to get back, because of his wife and the *Bazar*.

"You drove me nuts," he sighed at the bus stop. "Temporary insanity. A wonderful insanity," he noted. "Wonderful. Insanity. But when I think how already at your age, see it really knocks me over. I just don't know what to think."

"Don't think," I told him.

"But I can't help it. . . ."

He wanted to think. A little while before in the woods he wasn't thinking about thinking.

"It's really awful. I could kick myself. I shouldn't have. I should have taken the responsibility, since you're . . . but you drove me crazy. You can't look at men the way you do, what do you expect, it's your fault too! Men are weak, they can't resist it when a girl looks at them that way. . . ."

We took the bus back to Porte de Vincennes and changed to the 115 there. I would get off at the Project, he would stay on, he wanted to try to get to the *Bazar* before it closed, so he could bring his wife something wrapped up in the store's paper.

"You got to forgive me. Got to forget the whole thing, yeah? Promise me. Promise me you won't look at men that way any more. Promise me not to do things like that any more. You never know who you could pick up. There are some real bastards. They're not all like me you know. . . ."

One moment of madness and your whole life is wrecked. . . . When I think how you're the same age as my daughter it gives me the chills."

A little while earlier it was making him more hot than cold.

I didn't feel the need to talk. I was a little groggy. We were jammed closer and closer together on the platform as more people got aboard.

"A cute kid like you, it would be a real shame. . . ."

I looked at him with a big smile on my face. The bus jolts threw us against each other, I let it, and I could feel him beginning to recuperate. They need time.

"The thought that you're gonna go do that with just any . . . that kills me . . . a pretty little body like you have."

He took advantage of a jolt to hold me against him. When my stop came he didn't have much morality left, he wasn't saying a word any more. I asked him, "Your daughter, that's Juliette Halloin?"

I had just time enough to see his mug freeze over. He muttered something while I was getting off, something like "You wouldn't—" I was gone. I looked at him from the sidewalk, there on his platform. He was green.

They're really a riot.

Besides not three days went by before he was giving me the eye again; I steered clear. Finally he asked me if I was mad and if I held it against him.

"Wasn't it nice out there?"

"I'm not complaining."

"Well then? . . ."

When do we go back, he actually said. He had the bug again. They just need a little rest period. I told him, "I followed your advice I'm turning over a new leaf."

[87]

"Yeah?" he said, not knowing how to take it, whether he should congratulate me or not.

"Yes, I don't lay for family men any more."

A man is a good thing but still there are limits.

He was furious. He left with his teeth clenched and his balls in an uproar. They're a riot.

I was pleased with myself; there are some pleasures that beat the pleasures of the flesh.

But what really cracked me up was the hens. They tickled me. From the time I started walking around in a terrific gingham skirt I had managed to get the parents to buy me at the *Prisunic* and shortened right up to the latest style, they gave me dirty looks; I wasn't the nice little mommy now. God knows what I was. I heard one of them say "The way she walks," and the other one answered "It won't be long," she was obviously not too well-informed; and the whole thing loud enough for me to hear, so I would be ashamed of myself. I don't know how I walked, but at least I wouldn't want it to be like them, they looked like they had lead in their ass, maybe that was all their stupidity sunk to the bottom. Good God how I hated those hens! how could such things live? Why aren't they in the zoo? Dragging around whining all day long, can't move ten feet without plopping down, clumping in little bunches in front of the shops like bunches of mussels I'm being polite, reciting their miseries to each other, what miseries? and at night it grouses about how knocked out it is, and just what in hell has it turned out all day I ask you aside from a few lousy meals? And some poor sucker not that he deserves any better, he has to break his back to buy some expensive machine on time to save it "work," they call it, work it always made the kids do anyway mostly, and afterwards it's just as tired, to the point where you'd think tiredness is their only real profession. I don't know anything as useless in the whole world as hens. Oh sure. It lays babies. Life is a real crazy puzzle when you think about it.

Anyway since René I always got a bang out of seeing them; in a way I had really screwed them all at once, fishing someone out of their own generation and making him appreciate the difference. When Papa René climbed into the sack with his helpmate that Saturday night after the *Bazar* and the cold bath it must have given him a swift pain. I don't know which one she is, but they're all the same, and when they looked at me as though they were stripping me I did the same to them, and I wasn't the one to look away first. René had given me that, anyway, even if he had managed to spoil a nice memory by not keeping his yap shut afterwards. Hell. The days come and go. The flesh is new each morning. The boys are light and smooth, and thank God with them the most talk you ever get is "Nine o'clock?" "Right."

In fact once, because of the sometimes excessive absence of conversation, I was the only girl to turn up, against four guys. The other girls all got hung up at home, it turned out. You don't always do what you want when you live with the family.

We hardly talked then either, in fact nobody said a word, we took off anyhow. It was a beautiful night, in June. Warm. I'll never regret it.

Now everybody lent me their scooters. Even by myself, even for the whole day. I had finally gotten there, and even better than I had hoped.

Chapter 6

BUT WHAT ABOUT GUIDO, would I recognize him now? So much water had gone under the bridge since. So much. Guido, Guido—I would call his name to see if it did anything. Sure I remembered everything, his teeth, his hand when he held me; the woods; the scooter leaning against the tree—the scooter leaning against the tree had really left its mark on me, all I had to do was see a scooter leaning against a tree and I wanted to lie right down, it was automatic. A chimpanzee could have had me with that gimmick, the scooter leaning against the tree.

And when he talked in Italian. Oh that, that had stuck. Not the words of course, I couldn't have repeated a single one of them, except *morire*, and he said that after, not during—not the words but the sound, that kind of stream flowing from his mouth, from his mouth that really said what it was all about better than any good clear sentence. That music, what Guido was saying without me understanding anything, it was all of life, there's no sentence that can sum that up. The rest, the way it felt. . . . I could still hear the birds singing, during it. I had felt lots of things since then, a body doesn't really have much of a memory. Skin changes.

I was on the machine. Being on the machine was really something, no doubt about it—I stepped on the gas I slowed down I turned, I was alone I was free, it was a real joy; just being on the machine was worth all the trouble, even if I didn't find Guido.

If I found him I would tell him Get on! and I would be the one to take him away. That's the great thing about scooters, like knights and cowboys with a woman on the back, or thrown over the pommel crossways. Even a girl on it, she feels like a man, so what a man must feel, even a fag must believe he has a pair, that explained a lot. The way I tore around. I could have snatched anything, a prize fighter.

You get to Sarcelles over a bridge, and all of a sudden, from a little bit above, you see the whole thing. Oh gosh! and I thought I lived in a development! Now this was a development! This was Project, this was the real Project of the Future! Buildings and buildings and buildings for miles and miles and miles. All alike. In rows. White. And more buildings. Buildings buildings buildings buildings

buildings buildings buildings buildings buildings buildings. Buildings. Buildings. And sky—an enormous sky. Sun. The buildings filled with sun, shining through them, coming out the other side. Enormous Park Areas, clean, gorgeous carpets, each one with its sign saying Respect and Encourage Respect for the Lawns and the Trees, which incidentally seemed to make more of an impression here than where we lived, people themselves were probably making progress along with architecture.

The shops were set all together in the middle of each rectangle of apartments, so that each lady would have to go the same number of steps to pick up her noodles. There was even justice in this place. There were some beautiful chalets a little way off, all made of glass, you could see the whole inside as you went by. One was a library, with wonderful modern tables and chairs; you sat down there and everybody could see you reading. Another one was wood to look like a country house, with "Youth and Culture Center" marked on it. The Youth was inside, boys and girls, you could see them laughing and having fun in broad daylight.

A person could do no evil here; any kid who played hookey, they would spot him right off, the only one his age outside at the wrong time; a robber would show from miles away, with his loot; anybody dirty, people would send him off to wash. And if you felt like having a kid, as far as I could see there was no way to do it except to go through city hall, which I hope for their sake was close by too. Now that's architecture. And how beautiful it was! I had never seen so many windows. It made me dizzy, on top of all that turning into the first right, the first left, the first right, the first left; I was in rue Paul-Valéry, I took rue Mallarmé, I turned onto Victor-Hugo, went down Paul-Claudel, and ended up in Valéry again and couldn't get out. Where were the dormitories, where were the workmen, where was Guido? Even if he had been looking for me too we could walk around a hundred years and never meet, unless we had a sailor's compass. But here all they had was binoculars, you could see inside the houses and I saw two of them looking across from one building to another watching each other watch each other. It's something to do, and besides it makes you think.

Verlaine again, I had already seen that one, I decided I'd do better heading straight and I ended up at a fence. The end. So there was an end. I turned around and headed in the other direction, the road got slushy, I was in the construction area. They were adding houses, a couple of dozen of them. You could see the carcass, the big concrete supports. Which would soon be gorgeous white buildings. "You, Guido, you're building these houses, you who were born on the hills . . ." There was a puff of warm, fragrant air. "Ragazza, ragazza." You, Guido, Gouiido!

"Guido what?"

"I don't know."

"Gouiiido! Gouiido!"

"Hey kid, ragazza, what did this Guido do to you that somebody else can't do?"

"Hey piccolina, want me to be your Guido?"

"If you stick around till the end of the day I'll call myself Guido all night long!"

I stood there in the sunlight in front of all those men, with my mascara on my eyes, I had put a whole boxful on, and my gingham skirt, my one possession, and I had grown some more since, they could see my thighs, the sun went through me, the light washed over me in waves, the men were laughing, Italians Arabs Spanish, and the fore-man, he was French, giving me a dirty look, I looked like I was hustling I stood out. The happy boys were laughing healthy laughter behind their show window back there with the smooth-faced girls; they would have told me to go wipe myself off. It was too bright, too bright. I was bare as a fish. I looked for shade, someplace, someplace dark, someplace to hide, I was panicky, a crazy panic, I couldn't find the scooter again, I didn't know where I had left it. Paul Valéry. Confusion and darkness. I wanted a tool shed, a woodshed, a broom closet, a doghouse, a cave. Confusion and darkness, confusion and darkness, confusion and dark-ness. I found the scooter near a lawn. Respect and En-courage Respect.

It was beautiful. Green, white. Orderly. You could feel organization. They had seen to everything to make people comfortable, they had asked themselves "What should we put in so that people are comfortable?" and they had put it in. They had even put variety in: four big towers to break up the line; little hills, accidents in the landscape, so it wouldn't be monotonous; there were no two chalets the same; they had thought of everything, you could see their thoughts so to speak, set down there, with good will, the desire to do right, the effort, the care, the industry, the intelligence, right down to the last little details. They must have been real proud, the people who had done it.

In the mornings, all the men came out of the buildings and went into Paris to work; a little later it was the children who took off to school, the buildings would empty out like rabbits; all that was left in the Project were the women, the old folks and the invalids, and then, according to Liliane, the construction workers would go up to the women; if it's true someone must notice, but anyway what would the women do when the workmen weren't there any more? At night all the husbands would go back into the buildings and find the tables set, neat, with nice plates, the apartment all clean and good and warm, and everything all set for a nice evening, my God, my God, perfection, God is a pure spirit infinitely perfect I finally understood it.

I stopped again on the bridge on my way home, I turned back to look at the City. You should never look back when you leave a city, you turn into a pillar of salt; that must be true, I couldn't decide, I never got tired of looking. The windows were starting to light up. How beautiful it was! I couldn't get enough. Sarcelles was God, here you could begin to believe he had created the world, because if it takes a workman to build a house, Amen.

When I got back our own Project looked poor to me, old-fashioned, a real antique. We were already yesterday, it moves so fast, so fast. Even the apartments across the way, the "big ones," looked like nothing. Twelve crummy sheds on a little lot. I certainly wouldn't cry over them any more.

I felt closed in, I almost gasped for air. If you want to stay satisfied you shouldn't go out and see the world.

I met Ethel. I tried to tell her. It's like God. Come on why bring in God, men can build things themselves. Oh no it's worse! Ethel laughed. I don't see why it makes you sad, if it's as beautiful as you say it is. Yes it is beautiful. Well then? What do you want?

Confusion and darkness.

You want people to be dirty? you want them to have lice? Tuberculosis?

I don't know what I want.

If somebody had looked into my heart in those days they would have found a hidden feeling, for Frédéric Lefranc. He wasn't like the others. He was more serious, more thoughtful. But for just that reason he didn't have anything to do with us. He had other things to do in life. That was what attracted me, those "other things"—how lucky he was! and how did he do it? But at the same time it attracted me it set him miles away from me, me who had nothing. Near him I was tongue-tied; whatever I could say would only have sounded stupid to him. It was Ethel I talked to, that was easier, we had gone through school together and sometimes we had even turned out to be in competition. At the time that used to make us enemies, now it brought us closer together. I think Ethel felt bad for my sake that I hadn't gone on; I was like someone you have to leave by the wayside because he's too weak, and there's nothing you can do for him; you keep turning around, you're ashamed of your own strength. Ethel was the only person in the world I could talk to about diagramming sentences; she would have liked to help me, lend me books, but what good would that have done? Anyhow I couldn't anymore. I was out of practice now. She told me that in a Socialist Country I could have kept on with school, even if my family were poorer than it was; in a Socialist Country everybody did what he was best at. I told her that at the Guidance they had tried to figure out what I should do, but they hadn't found anything. She told me that was because they had only suggested jobs that would fit my parents' situation, which required me to earn a living right away; in a Socialist Country they wouldn't have considered that, only my interests and my abilities. I said that then it was like on Mars, and I started telling her that when I was a kid I had invented a planet Mars where everybody understood each other without even talking just by looking at each other, and where the trees never lost their leaves, and where . . . She said that was Escapism, that a person shouldn't indulge in Escapism, that my planet Mars was right here I had to make it. Her little serious side always hit you on the head just when you were starting to fool around, she was no good when it came to having a little fun. She was very nice, she tried to explain. But I wasn't as smart as she was, I hadn't gone to school long enough, it wasn't my fault. Past a certain point I would give up. And anyway, whenever I started thinking about serious things it would make me sad. When she asked me for the twentieth time, "Really, though, what do you want?" I started to cry. She took me home for dinner at their house to make me feel better; I didn't wait for her to ask twice, just the idea of seeing Frédéric and I got feeling happy as a lark again. Jeannot made a custard. What really got me about the Lefrancs was that the two boys, the younger ones, Jean and Marc, took care of the cooking, they did the dishes, and on top of that they seemed to think it was natural. I said in our house it wasn't like that, nobody ever even thought of asking them. "But why not? They have two hands, don't they?" Madame Lefranc said. I thought to myself I would be smart to import the system into our house, if it wasn't too late; I remembered once when mama tried to recruit Patrick, for a change, and with kid gloves at that—none of the girls were free—and how he had told her to go take a crap in terms I wouldn't dare repeat, and finished up by saying "Papa says that's not my job." Just what was his job I'd like to know. Anyhow so mama backed down, and papa confirmed the principle.

"Ten thousand apartments, all with hot water and bathrooms! That's really something!" Ethel was saying.

They were talking about Sarcelles, I had told them about my trip there.

"Yes," said Monsieur Lefranc.

"Yes," Frédéric said after him.

"You don't sound very enthusiastic," Ethel said.

"Sure I am," said her father.

"Sure, of course," said the son. "That's very nice."

"It certainly is very nice!" Ethel said. "Some people still live piled up six to a room in a hotel with a gas burner to cook on. I know some."

"Even you lived that way," her father said. "You don't remember, you were six months old when we moved."

"Those were some first six months," said her mother.

"I remember," Frédéric said. "It looked out over a filthy courtyard that stank."

"We lived in the 13th before this," I said. "There were rats there. I remember how scared I was."

"I was born in a cellar," Madame Lefranc said. "Now that I look back I don't really think I saw the sun before the age of reason. My mother had fourteen children, she has four left. In those days it was a terrible problem for a man to feed his family, he had to fight. . . . I remember how furious my father was," she said with a smile. "And the strikes . . . the unemployment . . . the riots. . . ."

"So?" Ethel said. "People are happier now, anyway, aren't they?"

"Yes," Frédéric said, "they're happier. . . ."

"Time out," Jeannot said. "How's my custard? You're all going to stuff it down without noticing."

That was true and it would have been a shame. His custard was terrific.

"Especially for a boy," I said.

"You can go on now," Jeannot said.

"But?"

"I didn't say but."

"You didn't say it but I heard it," Ethel said.

"Fine," Frédéric said. "But."

"People aren't any happier?" she insisted. Ethel never let go.

"Sure they are," Frédéric said, a little distant.

"Your discussion is really fascinating," Marc said.

"You're darn right it's fascinating," the father said. "Go on."

"Go on, brud," Marc said. "Up and at 'em."

"If happiness consists in accumulating household gadgets and not giving a good goddam about the rest of it, sure they're happy!" Frédéric burst out. "And all the time the manufacturers keep their junk moving with plenty of advertising and plenty of credit, and all is for the best in the best of all possible worlds. . . ."

"Capitalist worlds," his father said.

"Comfort isn't happiness!" Frédéric said, all wound up.

"What is happiness?" Ethel said.

"I don't know," Frédéric growled.

"But tell me, the fact that we've gotten to the stage where we ask ourselves this kind of question instead of how are we going to eat, doesn't that prove we've moved a little bit forward anyway?" Monsieur Lefranc said.

"Maybe," Frédéric said. "Yes, maybe, when you come right down to it."

"It takes having a taste of it to discover that comfort doesn't make happiness, doesn't it? It's a question of time. . . . When everyone has it, they'll wind up asking themselves the question. We've got to look ahead a little. I probably won't live to see that, but you will."

"Actually, happiness is living in the future. . . ."

He smiled a beautiful smile at me when he said that. And he probably really was living in the future, because as nice as he was he didn't seem to notice the looks I was giving him, or the fact that my shirt was open down to the next-to-last button, which was something the other boys would see first thing. And the other side of the coin is, usually they never see anything else. Probably when everybody on earth was happy he would begin to be interested in those things. Living in the future must have been a family thing anyway, Ethel didn't go with boys, either.

"I'll go with a boy I love for real," she would say. "Otherwise, why do it?"

Why. Now there was a question I really never asked myself before. Why. I had gone ahead and done it first. And, as I told Ethel, I didn't regret it, it hadn't done me any harm, and I was ahead by that much.

Anyway I would willingly have "gone" with Frédéric. But he didn't ask me. And he left for the Service. And he was killed.

* * * * *

Summer was ending. It was raining buckets. No more rides, no more stars. And it was Joël's turn to leave. I was beginning to hear talk of the army around me, it was a sign I was growing old. Patrick might go before draft age, they had warned him, if he didn't shape up he would be sent as a volunteer. He had gotten himself picked up for the first time—car theft. Everybody had seen it coming for a long time, they had told him often enough from the time he was a little kid how he would come to a bad end, since he wasn't too bright he couldn't miss getting pinched the minute he made a move. That's what happened. They held him long enough to teach him a lesson and sent him back to us, papa got to feeling sorry for him. But they kept an eye on him. One wrong step and he wouldn't get off so easy, said the judge, who was darned nice and easygoing I thought; I would have been meaner, I would have sent him off someplace to break rocks. That would have given him a little muscle besides; because too bad for him, that tough guy wasn't growing, not in height or in width. It drove him out of his mind, and no one did a thing to help him feel any better about it. Wait, I would say when something had to come down from a shelf, I'll get it for you, you could never reach it; I was always ready to do him a little favor when it came to that kind of thing, and so were the twins. Both of them were taller than he was by the whole height of their crinkly hair, and they were each half again as wide as him, which made them three against one, Patrick never considered laying a hand on them now. It was becoming clearer and clearer that they were not "of our blood," because where the folks were kind of slight these two were real heavyweights, they must have come down from Genghis Khan. But they were still with us, there was no more talk about the Substitution Affair; the folks had given up on it, they realized that it's only the people with pull who manage to get their rights, the ones in a position to get themselves talked about in the papers; they didn't know anyone or how to go about it; there's nothing but injustice and favoritism in life, those who have get. So the twins stayed and didn't let anyone push them around, in fact we hardly ever saw them, they were apprenticing and the rest of the time they led their own lives with their own friends. They were in a hurry to work for real, and to get out, and they didn't make any secret of the fact, "the ungrateful brats," mama said, it was true they wouldn't bring in much. Peace be with them. Patrick was worth even less, from the time the parents tried to get him out working they had to pay for damages instead of pocketing the salary. As the folks said it's pure self-sacrifice having kids for all you get out of it when they grow up. Should have told me ahead of time it was for an investment, Patrick retorted with good reason; I wouldn't have come.

"Too late now," Nicolas said, "you're here and you're screwing yourself, and you're gonna screw yourself the rest of your life, specially with the puss you got."

"Look you did I ask you the time of day?" But Patrick never went past talk with Nicolas, who was a lot tougher than he was.

"Quit looking cross-eyed," Nicolas said. "Makes you uglier than ever."

"Me cross-eyed?"

That was the kind of thing Nicolas was always thinking up; once he managed to make papa believe he was limping.

"I am not," said Patrick, who had gone to look in the mirror.

"If you're cross-eyed how can you see it when you look at yourself you big stupe!"

"Nicolas, I told you before don't talk like that didn't I?" mama said.

"Sure you told me before," Nicolas answered calmly as he went on drawing. He was drawing a big red picture with the title in huge letters: "The King the Queen and the Little Princes Decapitated by Me." I thought maybe he was going to be a great artist, but he told me he was going to be a Great Murderer.

"You'll see," he told me. "Just wait till I'm exactly as big as you. There's one thing I'm gonna do first, and then I'll be a Great Murderer."

Nicolas was in a hurry to grow up. Every morning he would measure himself and make a mark on the wall. He ate lots of soup, because he had heard it makes people grow. I never saw a kid each so much soup.

He wrote "I will kill my father. I will kill my mother. I will kill my brother. I will not kill my sister Jo I will love her a lot and I will tie her up with ropes, she will never go out again. I will bring her big steaks to eat."

When I was a kid I used to write things on little pieces of paper too. Not now. Now I sat for hours in front of the window pretending to sew, watching the rain fall, and the people go in and out the gate. We could see the gate now, we were in a different building; we had gotten a bigger apartment because of a larger family: ten living not counting Catherine, and one in the works, maybe even two if the doctor turned out to be right. Nobody had too much faith in him after the other time but they put it down on the application, might as well take advantage of it. We had four rooms. I would go into the front room and look as if I were sewing, I would watch the rain, and the people. They were people. It was rain. I was empty. The buildings

across the way didn't scare me, the boys didn't make me
burn any more, things were falling into place I don't know,
they didn't get into my heart the way they used to, wound-
ing me and hurting. Hurt, lovely hurt, come back! My head
was like a block of cement. Like when they say "There's
a fog, it won't clear up all day." It won't clear up. I had
come to a kind of dead end of my life. And when I turned
around I saw that behind me was a dead end too. Where
I was going? "Where are you going?" "Nowhere." "Where
do you come from?" "Nowhere." Jo! Jo of Bagnolet! A great
wind, my voice calling to me in the wilderness, I was not
answering. I never answered. "Where is little Jo?" I could
see myself so small, moving back and forth through the
gate with my shopping bag, tiny little girl in the midst of
the big buildings, and where was I going all dressed up
like that? Nowhere. When a person dies he sees his whole
life pass before him in a flash, I would die alone in the
midst of big buildings. Buildings buildings buildings buildings. How can you live in a world of buildings? "Guido
is it you, building these houses, you who were born on the
hills?" Phrases came and went, there were some that came
from behind, I would turn around, there was no one there.
Jo! "If a person has a soul he goes insane, and that's what's
happening to me." That was probably what was happening
to me I was going insane, no I was going dead, that's what
it was to grow up now I had it I was beginning to catch
on, getting into a dead end and starting to jell, with an
apron to mend eternally across my knees. Man is composed
of a body and a soul, the body is walled up into buildings,
the soul gallops over the hills, where? Somewhere there
was something I would not have because I didn't know
what it was. Once there had been something that didn't

Chapter 7

PHILIPPE. MY LOVE. WE CAME
to love each other little by little. Or it was more that we
were in love from the first moment we saw each other, we
realized that later, we both remembered it perfectly, that
day in front of the mailboxes, him with his dazed look, me
with the twins. The watchman. Papa. The drink. And if it
took a while for the thunderclap to get to us, that was
because of the silliest mistake: seeing me coming home
from the hospital, with newborn babies, and a man with

me, Philippe never figured for a second that the babies might not be mine. I remembered the way he stared at me, it certainly had seemed odd; that was because he was thinking Such a young girl with such an old man, and twins already! It stunned him. "And you were so beautiful!" he said. "You can't imagine how beautiful you were, with that baby in your arms, so little, tiny like you, what do you expect it just seemed logical that at your age you would have miniature babies!" He had even thought I looked like a young mother, happy and glowing, and he went as far as to say to himself What a shame it's not me instead of that old man! He was jealous of papa! It's crazy. And me with no idea what was going on in his head. So anyway he just came up with this crazy story, and right from the start, no really life is nuts. Consequence, a whole winter wasted, during which whenever we passed he would greet me with a very respectful Bonjour Madame, and all that time I thought he was shy, I would think my gosh what a screwball that guy is, he must be an idiot, and I went on stewing in sadness never guessing that happiness was right under my nose. Until the day he got up the nerve to ask me, still very respectfully, how my charming little babies Caroline and Isabelle were, he even remembered the names. Caroline and Isabelle were fine they had brought in the Cognac Prize and Philippe felt even better when he understood that they were my sisters, he couldn't believe it he asked me if I was really sure he made me repeat it four times and then, well, he didn't lose a minute asking me to go to the movies, and for that same night, and it didn't take me any longer to drop the whole gang, I wasn't so fascinated any more anyhow, we all knew everything there was to know about each other by now, it was getting to be routine, and besides the winter hadn't been too good, rides in wintertime aren't such a ball, there's no place to go, you can't strip, it's wet on the ground, it's cold, and I must say that when we managed to dig up a room somewhere well it just wasn't the same thing between four walls, it was a drag. We needed Nature, that's all there was to it.

In fact I even wonder if it wasn't Nature that made the whole thing, it's hard to express it. I wouldn't go so far as to claim it was the stars screwing me but that has something to do with it, and the proof is that with no stars, with an electric light bulb, it lost most of its appeal, it even got to be a little cruddy, there'd be too much drinking, and when I drink too much I feel things less, and the next day I feel rotten. Anyway to get back to Philippe we went to the movies, and he held my hand.

At the door coming home he told me he loved me.

"I love you," he said.

And he left. I almost said "What?" because he spoke in such a low voice I wasn't sure I heard him, but he was already gone. He lived in the F building, I lived in C. He had kissed me for an hour in front of my door, he said good night and to tell me good night he kissed me again, he hugged me against him so hard I almost smothered, all along I was expecting him to say "Come with me," and instead he said "I love you" and went away, leaving me there cold like a loaf of bread. He certainly wasn't like the others either, this guy; in a way he reminded me of Frédéric, at least his morals.

With the boys, we practically never kissed; just in the movies and even then the hands were always working too.

We didn't go for it much. Philippe had whiskers besides, he really scratched, my face was burning up.

We had a date for the next Sunday; I was really dropping the gang, that was for sure.

That Sunday he was waiting for me at the gate in a 2CV. He had just bought it, secondhand and on time, and from what he said it was on purpose for me, to take me out in. That seemed to mean he planned to take me out a certain number of times, otherwise he wouldn't take on such an expense.

Why was it such a wonderful thing just walking with Philippe, side by side with our fingers holding? Why him? And he was asking himself why her? We couldn't get over it either of us, that it should be us and nobody else. The funny thing was that we managed to meet at all. The idea that we just happened to live in the same place, when there are so many places. America. Even without going so far he could have been at Sarcelles for instance, and that would have been that. I would never have seen him, I wouldn't even know he existed and he wouldn't know I did. Just the thought of such a catastrophe terrified us, looking back— that we could have missed each other, each of us gone on living his own life like an idiot, and we were living like idiots both of us till now no point pretending any different, and besides we had always felt it deep down inside us, without knowing what it was we both lacked, it was The Other One. That was why I was sad so often, and cried for no reason, and ran around in circles not knowing what to do with myself, looking at the buildings, wondering why this why that, why the world and all the bother, making problems for myself and sitting in a trance behind a window, that was why that was why, and that was why I went with so many boys never caring who they were, since it was never the right one anyway, just to kill time while I waited for the only one on earth for me and now by some kind of fantastic luck he was here, beside me, his fingers twined in mine, and the proof that it was true was that for him I was the only one alive on earth, the one he had waited for living like a crazy fool his own way and now I was here with my fingers twined in his, bingo. Life is really pretty terrific when you think about it, everything happens that's supposed to happen, there's a certain logic to it. From now on we knew why the sun shone, it was for us, and that was why spring began too, just today, just when we were taking our first ride together, our first trip in love.

He stopped and said "Listen, a bird!" The song lifted through the cool air, into the bright sky. It was our bird. It was our sun. Our hawthorne all in flower, and there was our violet, our lily-of-the-valley sprout, still just a green point hardly there at all but we saw it, it was the first. Ours. The first in the world. Ours forever. Ah.

We walked through the woods that were still nearly bare, we walked hand in hand with the carpet of old leaves beneath our feet. We weren't in any hurry, we had plenty of time. Plenty of time. Time belonged to us too because we had eternity ahead of us. Everything belonged to us. It's crazy. Every three steps we would stop to look at each other.

"Jo. . . ."

"Philippe. . . ."

Our looks, our names, that would have been enough for us, almost enough, if we could have, if we had had the strength, I would so much have wanted that to be enough, for us to stay like that forever and ever, eyes gazing into eyes like two mirrors facing, it was so much more beautiful if only it could be, but the flesh is so determined, we wanted to touch, and when we touched we wanted to hold, we staggered, drunk with love, we went staggering toward a predestined joy that we had no power to resist despite the Perfection of What We Already Possessed and would have been so sweet to prolong. But it was impossible, we couldn't stand up any longer, our legs wouldn't carry us, the ground welcomed us like a great marriage bed, it was time, we couldn't hold out any longer.

"Jo. . . ."

"Philippe. . . ."

Only our Names, they said It All.

"Philippe."

"Jo."

"Ah."

From the moment he took me I was happy. It was such a long time since he had left me at my door burning. Four days. A woman can't wait. I was wildly happy. He was the one, he was really the one, just as I suspected, he was made for me, his place was waiting for him since forever. Afterwards he said to me, "Of course I'd like to have been the first. . . ."

He gave me a little smile, a bit sad, he was playing mechanically with last year's leaves.

"You're so young . . . I almost hoped."

First he thinks I'm a mother, then he wants me to be a virgin. My Philippe, he's marvelous. I stroked his cheek. He turned away a little angry.

"I love you."

He threw his leaves up into the air.

"Well that's just too bad! I should have gotten here sooner, it's my own fault."

Now I understood Ethel. Basically she was right. You should keep yourself for the boy you really love, that way there's no trouble.

"Philippe . . ."

"Jo!" He held me hard. "It doesn't matter," he said. "Now I have you, let's forget the past, life is starting out fresh right now I'm going to block them out," he murmured under his breath, growing again.

We stayed there all afternoon. We never got tired. We always wanted to. We would think we couldn't any more, and then we wanted to again. We rolled ourselves up in the blanket he had brought from the car just by chance I suppose. We saw each other. He was beautiful, every muscle of his body was beautiful, I wanted to kiss him all over. He did too. The cold chased us away. The sun was going down. Our sun was leaving us, even love couldn't keep the sun from setting. My skin was raw from his kisses and his bites, I had his mark on me and it kept me warm.

We were staggering again but this time it was from exhaustion, it was like we were drunk. When you make love you're always drunk, either from too little or too much. Then we realized we were dying of hunger; we had forgotten to eat. We couldn't get over it—my God did we make love! But now we were famished! Loving makes you hungry; it takes your appetite away, it gives you an appetite, love does everything, love is life full strength. "What would you like to do in life?" Love. Love, that's it, that's what I should have answered at the Guidance session. What did I want to do in life? Love. It turns out to be so simple.

Before we got back in the car he pulled me against him and took my face tenderly between his two hands. "Did I block them out?" he asked.

I almost asked who. God knows how far they were from my thoughts! There was nothing in my mind now but Philippe. Philippe Philippe.

"Philippe. . . ."

"Jo. . . ."

He kissed me.

"Well did I block them out?"

"What do you think . . . in the first place that wouldn't be hard—"

"Jo. . . ."

"—and besides I have no memory."

"You'll remember me, though, won't you? You're not going to forget me?"

"It's not the same with you. You're you."

"Jo."

"Philippe. . . ."

"Anyhow I won't give you any time to forget me! I won't let go of you. You know I'm never letting go of you again?" he asked me with infinite tenderness. "This is for good you know."

"Philippe."

"Jo."

"Philippe."

"My darling. You belong to me?"

"Yes."

"Forever?"

"Philippe my love."

"Jo my darling. How happy we're going to be!"

Happy?

"And how, we're going to be happy. It's hard for you to believe it huh my poor darling? You haven't had such a hot life, huh? my poor little love. But that's over now it's over I'm here, don't be sad, I'm here you'll see, I'm here now. Nothing will happen to you any more."

He was twenty-two years old. He was a television installation man. He had just started to work for a big shop, with a future. He would earn a good living. They were five children, the oldest daughter was married, the second one was working, steno, the last two kids would be getting along on their own soon, the mother was dead. He wouldn't have too many responsibilities. He still lived with them, but he had applied for an apartment and made up his file already. He had done his Service, he had come back the past fall, that was why I hadn't seen him before. He never talked about what it was like down there. He didn't want to talk about it. He never never wanted to think about it again, ever. Not about that, or any of the rest of it, he was sick of all that stuff, he didn't want to get involved. In any of it. Just be happy, that's all, the one thing a person has to do in life is be happy, there's nothing else, nothing, and to be happy you've got to love, you've got to be two people who live for each other without paying any attention to the other stuff, who build a nest to hide their happiness in and protect it from attack.

When I told him I was pregnant, and it shouldn't have

been any surprise it had to happen with our methods, we could never separate and we even put it back in the excitement of the moment there's nothing more dangerous than that poor Liliane had told me that, in fact with all her information it hadn't done her any good she had died and in a rotten way the poor girl, that scared me, but when I told Philippe he picked me up and swung me around in the air like a nut. I really like that better.

"From the first day I saw you with a baby in your arms that's what I wanted," he yelled. "You just don't know! Starting that day I wanted to make you a baby!"

He told me that every time he made love to me he thought about it, he would keep telling himself I'm making her a baby, right this minute I'm making a baby in her, and that would drive him crazy with joy, with happiness, with pleasure. The idea of making me a baby would make him come. Well, there it was, made, he hadn't come for nothing.

That was all he had been waiting for, he said, to get married for real. And fast now. Not for the principle he didn't care about that he was broad-minded, but he wanted me still to look slim when I came out of the city hall with him holding my arm; really beautiful, in a beautiful dress he would buy me, not white of course that was kid stuff it didn't matter, but a beautiful dress, something I had never had. He wanted to have a beautiful memory of that day to keep in his heart.

We would buy a cradle. He was already looking at them in the windows. He didn't want any lousy bed, the kind of thing that's so-called useful for later, never mind the expense, he wanted a cradle a real one, with the organdy thing that hangs around it outside. Blue. No, pink, because he wanted a little girl. It's true they're more practical.

Anyway, as far as the maternity grant went we would be inside the time limit.

The important thing was finding a place to live and pronto; we would have to get the application moving, we could look on our own too, his company would certainly let him have a loan, on time, and anyhow there was always the Credit. By now there were beginning to be places where you could find something. I suggested Sarcelles.